KATRINA CAPPELLI

Midnights

TIME WON'T FLY BOOK ONE

To Francesco,

I hope my writing journey inspires you to follow your dreams sooner than I did. Know I will always be there to support you, just like your mom was there for me.

More From the Author

Stand-alone Books:

Stars & Margaritas

Time Won't Fly Series:

Midnights

Lavender Haze Sunrise (Coming Soon)

Content Warning

This book contains explicit, on-page sexual content, and is intended for adult readers (18+). However, it has been written so that you can easily skip those scenes if you are uncomfortable with them or related to me.

Skip the following chapters if you want to omit the explicit content:

Chapter 12

CHAPTER 1

"Welcome to the Cosimo Tech Summit, or as I like to call it, your glimpse into the future," I say to the invisible audience in my bedroom mirror. "I am Ace Cosimo, and I will be walking you through our latest development here at Cosimo Tech."

I take a rehearsed beat and flip to my next flashcard. "And this technology…" Wait. That's not right. I flip through the rest of my cards to see if they're in jumbled order, but they are fine. I'm just missing one.

I turn around and scan the room. It shouldn't be that hard to find a bright pink note card in a room that has a white colour palette. I was working on them before I went to sleep. It's likely hidden somewhere in my unmade king-size bed. I climb into it and move all the sheets around to look for the elusive card. No luck. I slide my hand down the back of the bed between the mattress and my imported wood headboard. Still not there.

This presentation had to be perfect. I had to find that card. How did it even get lost? It is highlighter pink. It's not even like the room is too dark to see it. The wall behind my bed is made up of floor to ceiling windows that look out over the ocean, and not to mention the skylight above. This is the brightest room in the house at this time of morning.

There is one place I haven't checked yet. Underneath the man currently sleeping in my bed. When I picked him up last night, I was kind of hoping he was one of those sneak-out-of-the-house-after-I-fell-asleep type. Evidently, he is the sleep-in-and-snore-because-he-has-nothing-else-to-do-on-a-weekday type. Honestly, the fact that my frantic search hasn't woken him up is impressive.

I could wake him up, but I feel like it would be rude considering I have no idea what his name is. Did he even tell me? There was a lot of "Oh yeah, baby, right there," last night and not a lot of calling him by his actual name.

His groan signals that I won't have to worry about waking him up any more. He turns to where I'm standing.

"Good morning," he says with a little smile.

"Sup. Any chance you are lying on a pink notecard?" I ask him. He rolls over a little and sure enough, there is a note card stuck to his abs.

He peels it off his six-pack, and it's like a core memory unlocks. His name is Joe. I remember hitting on him by saying, "Joe Six-pack." Man, it's a good thing I'm pretty because I have no game.

He hands me the note card. "What time is it?" he asks.

I pick up my phone to check the time. Shit. I'm running late. If I don't catch Eli, he'll leave without me.

"Time for you to leave." No time for morning pillow talk, I start picking his clothes up off the ground and throwing them at him.

As he gets dressed, he starts to talk. Something about the house being nice, I don't know. I'm tuning him out as I guide him out of my room, down the stairs, and out the front door.

I'm about to shut the door behind him, when he turns around and stops me. "I didn't get your number," he says, leaning on the door frame like his mere presence is supposed to impress me.

"Yeah, okay. Bye," I say as I shut the door in his face. I do not have time to babysit my booty call. Frankly, he wasn't that great, I'm not in the market for a repeat performance.

I walk into the sleek modern kitchen and find our housekeeper, Joy, making breakfast. She puts a plate of eggs and bacon in front of me as I sit down at the island.

"I see you took your own trash out," she comments. For such a tiny woman she holds a lot of rage. Not one thing has changed about her appearance since I first met her at six-years-old. I remember with her black bob and penchant for the colour black, I was convinced she was a vampire. To this day I'm not entirely unconvinced that she's not.

"I assume you will be washing your own sheets tonight."

Joy refuses to clean up after me ever since she found a used condom in my room. Which, to be fair, is disgusting, but in my defense, the guy told me he threw it away and it was hidden under some clothes.

"Yes, I will, but not tonight. Eli and I are going to Vegas for the Summit," I say as I dig into my eggs.

"Oh, that's why you look different," Joy says.

I look down at my outfit to see what she's talking about. Dressing professionally isn't my forte, so I had my friend Natalie pick something out. I'm wearing a pencil skirt, with a white blouse and a blazer, instead of my usual jeans and t-shirt. My auburn hair is pulled back into a sleek ponytail, rather than a messy bun, and I'm wearing glasses instead of contacts. According to Natalie, wearing my glasses will help me look smart, because apparently, presenting ground-breaking technology that I helped create isn't enough.

"I wanted to look the part so people didn't think I was some kind of nepotism hire," I explain.

"But you are a nepotism hire." I glare up at Joy.

She's not wrong. I'm Eli's daughter, but no one

else knows that. When I came to live with Eli after my mom died, it was decided that it would look better if Eli said I was a distant cousin that he took in out of the kindness of his heart, instead of the daughter it took him six years to finally take responsibility for.

Where Joy's wrong is that anyone who knows Eli, knows that he isn't one to give handouts. Everything has to be earned, and Eli's form of currency is knowledge. It wasn't until I got kicked out of boarding school for blowing up the chemistry lab that Eli took an interest in me.

I still remember the meeting in the headmaster's office. "I don't understand how she can be held responsible when you are teaching the students these volatile chemical reactions," Eli said to the headmaster. To which the headmaster explained that the reaction I had created wasn't part of the curriculum.

Eli turned to me and looked very serious. His only question was "Were you trying to make it explode or was it an accident?" I explained to him the exact reason I mixed together the chemicals was to create the desired effect of an explosion. It was then that everything changed.

Eli took me back home and hired tutors. I had finished high school by sixteen and then was enrolled at MIT which I graduated from at nineteen. After a brief stint in the military, I went to work in research and development for Cosimo Tech. I've been with the company almost six years now and this latest project is my first time co-leading with Eli. If I nail this presentation, then maybe I can be respectable enough in Eli's eyes to be his full-fledged daughter. If I could just make him proud enough, then maybe he'll finally tell the world.

A loud crash comes from below, pulling me from my thoughts. Joy and I both look at the door to the basement where the home lab is. It flies open and Eli enters the room. His white hair is askew, his usually neatly trimmed beard is looking a little scruffy, and he is wearing the outfit he wore yesterday. I specifically remember the assault on my eyes that the pattern on his pants waged. He looks like some kind of mad scientist.

"You look like shit," I tell him as he sits next to me at the island.

"Good morning to you too, Ace," he says,

taking his plate of breakfast from Joy.

"Were you in the lab all night?" I ask.

"No, I just woke up early," he answers.

I look at Joy questioningly, and she shakes her head, confirming my suspicion. Eli has been spending most nights in the lab lately.

"What are you working on?"

"None of your business." It's typical for Eli to be defensive about his work, but usually he at least tells me what it was he's working on so he can try to trick me into helping him. He's never needed to trick me. I'll always help him but his ego keeps him from asking me directly.

"If you tell me what it is, I can help you," I say, seeing if the little nudge would make him open up.

"If I need your help, I will ask," he replies pointedly.

We sit in silence as I let him cool off for a moment. I wrack my brain for what he could be working on. Eli made his fortune by developing a mechanical prosthetic that used neuro-transmitters to allow the user to move the limb using brain signals. Since then, the niche for Cosimo Tech had always been technology with ties to the human brain.

Within the last couple of years, Eli has started toying with the idea of time, tying it with his knowledge of the brain in our most recent project, the Time Keeper App. A VR app that works with updated versions of our neuro-transmitters to allow you to relive your memories. As we wrapped up the project over the last couple months, Eli's interest in time has slowly turned into obsession, and I'm sure it isn't a coincidence that it coincides with the death of his wife, Odette.

"You know, if you are working on improvements to the Time Keeper App, it might be a good idea to incorporate them into our presentation today." He'd mentioned something about making the memories more real a few weeks ago. I shut the idea down because it was too big of a can of worms to open that close to launch. It would make sense that he wouldn't tell me if he was working on it on his own.

"Our presentation?" Eli asks with a mouth full of eggs.

"Yes, the one we are giving at the Summit," I answer.

"You aren't going to the Summit," he says as

he pushes his half eaten plate of eggs away from him and stands. He starts to head for the door and I grab a piece of bacon off my plate before following.

"What do you mean I'm not going? We developed the Time Keeper App together. I should be in on the presentation," I yell after him.

"The people come to the Summit to see me, Ace."

"What if they start coming to see both of us? They don't even know me yet," I argue.

He stops and turns around to face me. "The real fans know you as my pseudo-daughter," he says.

"What?" I ask.

"You have been living with me since you were six. You're like my adopted daughter. My real fans know that," he explains.

I open my mouth to speak but close it again, trying to process exactly what he is saying. "But I am your actual daughter."

"Sure, kid," he says as he takes the bacon strip out of my hand. "I'll see you tomorrow." He puts the bacon in his mouth and heads out the front door.

I just stand there, baconless, staring at the closed door, wondering what the hell my next move is.

CHAPTER 2

"It's bullshit that he left you out of that presentation," Natalie says over the loud music at our favourite bar. I've just finished telling her about what happened this morning, leaving out a few of the details. She, like the rest of the world, is under the impression that I'm Eli's cousin, not his daughter.

Natalie's older than me, but not wiser. We met in Boston—she was attending Harvard Medical School while I was at MIT. She found a residency in Malibu and we became even closer friends. A few years ago, Cosimo Tech needed another neurologist on staff and, through some gentle nudging on my part, Natalie got the job.

"I don't want to talk about it," I tell her as I toss back my third shot of tequila. Now that I'm done venting, I just need to forget this day ever happened. I knew Natalie would be understanding of at least some of it, since she worked on the project, but no one could understand the full extent of my disappointment. That's where the drinks came in.

"You should just tell him that he's an asshole," Natalie advises, taking her own shot of tequila. She's not wrong, but Eli is fragile, and the only family I have. If I piss him off, I'll end up all alone.

"I said I don't want to talk about it." I turn around and lean back against the wooden bar to emphasize my point. I look out at the rest of the place. It's kind of a dive, but that's why we like it. The space is filled with pool tables and air hockey tables. It's a busy night, so most of them are in use.

"Fine, we don't have to talk about it," Natalie concedes and turns to lean against the bar next to me. "Any talent here tonight?"

I scan the crowd to see if anyone catches my

eye. After getting passed over this morning, I'm not in the mood to spend the night alone in the mansion. With Eli out of town, Joy won't be around either. I'm a fan of sleeping alone on a good day, let alone a crappy one.

Usually, all it takes is some eye contact and a hair flip to get a cute guy to come over to us. We both look hot tonight, Natalie's curly blonde hair is down and she has the perfect shade of red lipstick on. I have my auburn hair in a high pony and I finally have the cat eye eyeliner down to a science. As Taylor Swift would say, it's sharp enough to kill a man, so my hazel eyes pop.

The cold air blowing through the open door catches my attention and the man coming through it takes my breath away. I must audibly gasp because Natalie's gaze follows mine and her reaction is not as positive. "No," she says, grabbing my chin to take my attention away from the bad decision.

"No, what?" I ask, pretending I don't know exactly who she's talking about.

"Going home with literally anybody else in this bar would be a better idea than what you are thinking right now," she answers.

She has a point, but something about the man who is walking toward us makes me forget why I should stay away.

Sawyer looks better than the last time I saw him. He's wearing a simple white t-shirt that hugs his muscular arms. His blonde hair is spiked a little and he must have been off for a few days because he looks like he hasn't shaved.

Before I know it, he's standing in front of me and I'm lost in those green eyes of his. "Hi, Ace," he says, and a shiver goes through my body. I always loved how he said my name.

"Hi, Captain," I reply, and see his perfectly stubbled jaw tense.

"You don't have to call me by my rank anymore," he corrects.

"I know, but I also know you like it when I do," I tease.

"It's nice of you to come say hi, but Ace and I are having a girls' night," Natalie cuts in. Neither of us look her way, completely locked in on each other.

"I didn't mean to interrupt," he says defensively.

"Then what brings you in? It's been a hot

minute since you have been here," I ask.

"I was feeling nostalgic. There are some things I miss about this place." I hold back my smile. I don't want him to know he's getting to me. "I heard about the amazing work you're doing at Cosimo. I just wanted to congratulate you."

"Well, now you have. We are going to go over there now." Natalie grabs my arm to take me to the other side of the bar. I stay planted, fully entranced by him. Sawyer is here to see me. He knew this is where I hang out and he hasn't come in here since we stopped seeing each other.

"I'd love to see what you are working on now. Watching you work was one of my favourite things," he says to me, ignoring Natalie.

"I don't know. I had my eye on something over there." I nod vaguely to the other side of the bar.

Sawyer turns to where I gestured and then looks back at me, green eyes smouldering. He put his arm on the bar behind me and leaned in close, whispering in my ear. "I don't know who you are talking about but I guarantee I can make you come faster."

His words made my brain short circuit,

remembering just how fast he could make me come.

"I'd love to show you what I've been working on," I say, and Natalie pulls on my arm.

She looks at me disapprovingly with raised eyebrows. She's worried because Sawyer and I didn't end well. I shrug back at her. There is something different about tonight. He's never sought me out before. It's always been me chasing him.

I turn to Sawyer. "Let's get out of here."

"Lead the way," he says, gesturing for me to head off in front of him.

I turn back to Natalie. "I'll call you tomorrow," I say, but she's giving me an 'are you fucking kidding me' look. "Just one second," I say to Sawyer as I pull my friend out of his earshot.

"What are you doing?" she asks.

"Look, I don't want to be in the house alone tonight. I'm going to have to spend the next hour pretending to be into a sports team to get any other man in here to go home with me. Plus, once I get them home, there is only a fifty percent chance they can actually get me to orgasm, and that is being generous. Sawyer is easy, and I am very sure he can get me over the finish line. That's all this is," I explain.

She doesn't look convinced. "So, you aren't reading in to the fact that he showed up at our favourite bar?" It almost hurts that she knows me so well, but doesn't at the same time. But thinking about that is just more of a reminder that I need a new plan to impress Eli. The exact thing I'm trying to forget about tonight.

"Nope, it's purely coincidental that he's here." I don't like lying to her, but I need a distraction and Sawyer is the perfect one.

I think Natalie sees the desperation in my eyes. "Fine," she says quietly, letting me go. It's moments like these she tows the line between friend and mom. Knowing she knows better than me, but also knowing that I have to make my own mistakes.

I didn't show Sawyer what I had been working on. We almost didn't make it to the bedroom before we were tearing each other's clothes off.

I turn to Sawyer lying next to me. He's out of

breath and flushed, coming down from the amazing sex we just had. I slide closer to him and rest my head on his chest.

I trace the shape of his six-pack with my fingers and look up into his captivating green eyes. "I'm having trouble remembering why we broke up," I say to him playfully.

"I mean…can you really call it a breakup if we were never in a relationship?"

Right. That's why we weren't together. Every time I suggested we were more, Sawyer always reminded me that it was just sex.

"Good point," I say. I didn't want to disagree with him and have him leave. The last thing I wanted to do was spend the night in this big house alone. I look down at what my fingers were doing, not being able to maintain eye contact anymore, so he wouldn't see the disappointment in mine. His hands stroked up and down my arm. An affectionate gesture that goes against everything he said with his words.

"You know; I really do want to check out what you are working on. It wasn't just a line to get you back here," he says.

"Eli has the proto-type. He's presenting it to shareholders," I answer. Even if the proto-type was here, I wouldn't have shown it to him. There's no way I'm letting him out of this bed until morning.

"There's nothing else you have going on in that basement lab of yours?" he asks.

This is weird. Sawyer has never shown any interest in my work. The only thing he used to be interested in doing in that basement was me.

"Eli's being weird about having people down there. Besides, we are between projects right now, anyway," I answer. I turn to look at him again, running my hand down the side of his face. "Let's just get some sleep."

He leans down to kiss me. "But I'm not tired," he says as he runs his hand down my body, cupping my ass. I kiss him back, and he uses his grip on me to shift us so he's on top of me.

"Well, what do you think we should do then, Captain?" I ask him, knowing that using his rank made him go feral. Back when we were sneaking around, we always used to find ourselves hidden away in a closet somewhere whenever I called him Captain.

"Oh, I have a few ideas," he answers, kissing me again, thoroughly distracted.

CHAPTER 3

I open my eyes to find the source of the incessant buzzing that is keeping me from being able to enjoy sleeping in on a Saturday. I look at my nightstand to see the screen of my phone lighting up.

I pick it up and check the caller ID. The screen says "Soup—do not answer."

I hit the button to stop the ringer and try to go back to sleep. I get two minutes of peace before the buzzing starts again.

With an eye roll, I resign to my fate and unplug

my phone. I quietly slip out of bed as to not wake Sawyer. The last thing I need is Soup finding out that he's here. I grab a t-shirt off the floor and throw it on before answering the phone in the hallway.

"Soup, it is six on a Saturday morning. What the hell do you want?" I say into the phone.

"I told you not to call me that," Soup replies on the other end of the line. His real name is Lawrence Campbell. He is a good friend of Eli's and the liaison for Cosimo Tech's military contract. He is also one of the few people who knows that Eli and I aren't cousins.

"Would you rather I called you Larry?" I counter.

"Honestly, anything would be better than Soup." Soup and I have never really gotten along, but the relationship has been more strained since I left the military.

"In that case, Soup it is." I hear a telltale groan come through the phone. "Did you call just to complain about your nickname? Because that could have waited until ten."

"No. One of my reports on base has a Cosimo prosthetic and his transmitter broke."

With Eli still out of town, it made sense that I was the one he called for this. We weren't exactly friends. He would never call me unless he needed something.

"Did you try tech support?" I ask, knowing he probably hadn't.

"I did, but they are only sending out the new transmitters, and his model is too old for it to be compatible. Does Eli have an old one in his lab? Just to hold him over until we can get his prosthetic upgraded?"

"Let me go look," I say with a sigh.

Usually, I would make him sweat a little before giving him what he wanted, but it's six in the morning and I just want to go back to bed. I make my way down to the basement lab. I haven't been down there in three months, not since Eli's wife died in a car accident. I've been trying to give Eli his space. When he is upset, he channels it into work.

Eli was a bit of a playboy when I was growing up, but that changed three years ago when he met Odette. I don't want to think about what she did to get him to commit, but one day he came home and introduced her to me as my new step-mom. Judging by the look on her face, she had no idea he had a kid—let alone one that was only a few years younger than her. We didn't interact much. She seemed to actively avoid me, and I wasn't about to go out of my way to spend time with someone who didn't want to spend time with me.

I make it to the door to the basement and give it a pull, but it doesn't budge. The house itself is secure, so Eli never really locked anything up inside. The door has a keypad lock. I try Odette's birthday, Eli's birthday, and their anniversary before taking a shot in the dark and trying my birthday. The keypad lights up green and the door unlocks.

I try not to read too much into the fact that my birthday is the code and head down the stairs. I really should have come down here sooner. It looks like a bomb went off. One side of the large room has tables with holographic interactive screens. Underneath the tables is storage for tools and parts, though currently, those tools and parts were scattered over every surface.

I walk up to the table that usually holds the bins with the transmitters, and the motion activates the display. I shift around the clutter on the desk and don't immediately look up. Already exasperated by the search for these stupid transmitters, I plop down in the closest chair. I finally notice what is displayed on the screen, it says "Resume Project: Out of Time."

I don't recognize the project name, and I should really respect Eli's privacy. But 'Out of Time' feels pretty ominous, considering the mental state that he is in. It would be irresponsible of me not to check out what it is.

I mute my phone so Soup can't hear.

"Resume," I say out loud for the voice command.

"Voice recognition failed. Passcode is required to continue," the automated voice replies. The default security when opening new files is set to allow Eli and me into them. He would have had to go out of his way to change the settings in order to lock me out. I mean, I have been hacking his passcodes since my boarding school days—being able to delete emails from the headmaster came in real handy sometimes—so it didn't really matter, but it's a little concerning that Eli would lock me out of a file.

I enter his password, and window after window opens with notes and schematics. I read through them. It all sounds like the ramblings of a man who has lost his mind. Things about the movement of time and the correlation between light and time. Eli could be a little erratic at times, but he always made sense.

The schematics are for a large machine. It consists of a round platform big enough for two people to stand on, with large arms curling up around them. The electrical wiring is complex, and the list of materials is long. Whatever the machine is will probably take him a long time to build. It's not time to worry yet.

I swivel in my chair towards the other side of the lab and see that it might actually be time to worry. The space that is usually open for building larger machinery now held the machine from the schematics. I walk over to it slowly, always best to be careful when you are not sure exactly what activates the thing or what it does. On one arm, there's a display screen. I touch it to wake it up and what I see makes me more confused. *Enter destination date.*

Is it some kind of teleportation device? Why would it need a date for the destination? Unless the date was the destination? Wait a second. He couldn't have. He didn't.

I run back to the desk and search through the files. I find an animated demonstration video that Eli made. I hit play and what happens makes me shudder.

It's a fucking time machine.

My internal freak out is interrupted by two pressing matters. I can hear Soup yelling on my phone and I can also hear my name being called from upstairs.

I pick up my phone and unmute it. "Soup, he doesn't have any. I'll come by the base tomorrow and recalibrate the prosthetic." Before Soup can answer, I hang up.

I make my way up the stairs and almost run into Sawyer at the top.

"There you are," he says as he wraps his arms around my waist.

"Yup, here I am," I reply.

He peeks past me down the stairs. "I thought you were between projects right now?"

Nope. I am done with his shit. It is early in the morning, Eli is doing something shady in the basement, and I had to talk to Soup before coffee. My patience has run out for the day. Sawyer has made it abundantly clear that we aren't a couple, so I have nothing to lose.

"What's going on? You have never shown any interest in what I was working on," I call him out.

"That's not true," he argues.

"Sawyer, I'm not an idiot. You haven't been to that bar in years because it is my favourite and you have been avoiding me. Just tell me what your game is," I say.

"Campbell is up to something and I think that Eli might be helping him," he explains, taking his hands off my waist and stepping back. He caved faster than I thought he would.

"What do you mean, Campbell is up to something?" I ask.

There is a possibility it is the time machine, but I doubt Soup would send me into the basement if he knew what was down there.

"He's been leading a special project. They pulled a couple of my guys for it and I haven't heard from them since." To Sawyer's credit, he looks genuinely upset. He isn't all bad, otherwise I wouldn't have fallen head over heels in love with him.

"The Cosimo prosthetic guys?" I ask. When I met Sawyer, he was running a team made up of soldiers that had lost limbs and had Cosimo prosthetics. It was a trial run and they have since been folded in to other places.

"No. None of them."

"Then what makes you think Eli is involved?" It wasn't a completely crazy thought. Part of our military contract required we provide them with new exclusive technology and the deadline is coming up, but if Eli is helping Soup with something, he would tell me.

"The only rumblings I've heard about the project is that it is science related. I know Cosimo Tech owes us some sort of technological advancement. I thought whatever Campbell is working on was it," he explains.

"Eli's not working with Campbell. He's been doing his own thing. I don't think he's even spoken to him since Odette's funeral," I tell him. It's the truth. At least I'm pretty sure it is. The progress Eli has made on his little side project would have taken him a long time. There was no way he also had the capacity to help Soup with whatever shady things he was doing.

Sawyer looks defeated. I feel bad for him for a whole five seconds until I really think through the whole situation.

"Why didn't you just ask me if Eli was involved? Why go to the bar and create this elaborate ruse?" I ask.

His eyes drift down my body in answer. I suddenly become very aware of the fact that I am only wearing a t-shirt. His t-shirt.

"Yeah. It's time for you to go." I turn him around and start guiding him towards the front door.

"I'm sorry, Ace. It's still early. Let's just go back to bed," he says, looking back at me with that damn sexy smirk of his.

"I have too much to do today," I reply, still pushing him towards the door.

"It's Saturday," he argues.

"There is no such thing as weekends in tech." I open the front door and gently push him out of it.

He turns around to face me. "I kind of need my shirt."

It takes a second for his words to register. I look at him and realize that this whole time he was only wearing pants and not a shirt.

I pull his shirt up over my head and throw it at him, oblivious to the fact that I'm naked underneath. The way his jaw hits the floor, he's not oblivious to my nakedness. It doesn't stop me from slamming the door in his face.

I turn around and lean back against the door, sliding down to sit on the floor. I close my eyes and take a deep breath. I didn't lie to Sawyer. I really do have a lot going on at the moment.

I need to get dressed and then figure out what the hell I am going to do about Eli's time machine.

When Eli arrives home, I am sitting in the lab with my feet up on the table, eating a bag of chips. He isn't exactly happy to see me.

"How did you get into the lab?" Eli asks as he storms over to me.

"I graduated from MIT at nineteen. You really think I can't get past a keypad and a password?" I reply.

He pushes my feet off the table. "What are you even doing down here?"

"That's funny. I was about to ask you the same question," I throw back at him.

The mood shifts, and Eli's gaze moves to the floor. "From your tone, it sounds like you already know." He sounds more defeated than I have ever heard him. "I guess you have been waiting down here to tell me to stop."

The truth is I had, but something about the pain in his eyes that I so rarely saw was making me pause. "We both know it's not a good idea to mess around with time. In every movie that deals with time travel, something always goes wrong," I say, trying to soften the blow.

"I only want to use it once. Then we can destroy the thing and never think about it again." His voice is quiet, and he is looking me in the eye again. The desperation there hurts my heart.

"What do you want to use it for?" I ask, though I have a feeling I already know the answer. I need to hear him say it.

"I want to bring her back."

Odette. I was indifferent to my stepmother. I was sad that she died. She was young, and it was tragic. But I didn't feel the loss. Not like Eli did.

"How are you going to do that? Stopping the car accident? We don't know how this stuff works. What if it goes all *Final Destination*, and she gets electrocuted in a tanning bed the next day? You going to fire up the time machine again?" I argue.

"Maybe. I'll cross that bridge when we come to it." I can see Eli putting his walls back up. He stops looking at me, turning his attention to some parts sitting on the table.

"What if it's something you can't fix? What if she gets sick?" He ignores me. "Eli, you can't just build a time machine."

"I already did!" Eli yells as he turns to face me again. He takes a breath and closes his eyes to calm himself down. I want so badly to tell him that going to therapy was likely a simpler solution to his grief, but I feel like I'm one comment away from being thrown out on my ass.

"Have you used it?" I ask calmly. I want to be gentle. Eli has never opened up to me before. This is unprecedented. I can't help myself from thinking that maybe this is us making strides, maybe the next step was announcing to the world who I really am.

"No, but it is ready for a test run." The anger

melts from Eli's face. His features soften, and he looks at the floor before he continues. "I know yesterday I said I didn't need your help, but I really could use you, Ace. Could you please help me out?"

Shit. I had a decision to make. I either help Eli with the time machine so the reckless asshole doesn't kill himself, or I leave him to his own devices and hope he doesn't burn down the world in the process.

I take a deep breath. My heart breaks for him. I really take him in. There are dark circles around his eyes, like he hasn't slept in weeks. His hair is pointing in about five different directions and his beard looks less intentional and more like he hasn't bothered to shave. He puts on a show and acts like he's fine, but right now the mask is off and I can see the grief that he has been hiding for the last three months.

He has never once asked me to help him with something. He always just assumes that I will. The closest he gets to asking is when he deliberately says something wrong and waits for me to correct him and take over. If I say no now, it is more than likely he will never ask again. We didn't always get along, but Eli is the only family I have, and I'm not about to push him away.

"Fine. I'll help you," I agree, and I almost immediately regret it. But it's too late. I'm in it now and there's no turning back. Maybe it wouldn't be bad. Maybe this will be the catalyst we need in our relationship. The thing that finally makes him see me as his family and not just a conveniently located assistant. It's worth a shot isn't it?

I try to avoid the soldier's sexy green eyes as I work on recalibrating his prosthetic arm. After some bad experiences, I made it a point to avoid messing around with guys in the army, especially those under Soup's command. His eyes also remind me of Sawyer, which is the last thing I need.

I make one last adjustment on the receiver and then move away from him to get a better look at the whole arm. I can't go far because the lab on the base is basically a glorified closet. The room is mostly full of shelves filled with old equipment and a small table in the corner where I have my small toolbox. The tight quarters don't help with my personal boundaries. He smells really good too.

"Can you try to move your fingers again?" I instruct the soldier.

He narrows his eyes, and the fingers on his prosthetic move. Relief fills his face as he tests out the movement of his entire arm. He looks up at me. "Thank you for coming down here."

I can't help but smile. I wave my hand at him, brushing off the compliment. "It was nothing."

He stands and moves closer to me. "Really, thank you. I thought I was going to have to go into surgery again and get a whole new arm."

"Well, you're welcome. I'm glad you didn't have to go into surgery." I smile at him. When I was in the military, I worked with a group of soldiers that had Cosimo prosthetics. Working in research now, I missed helping people. I know my work still helps people, but there is something about one-on-one interactions.

The soldier takes another step closer to me. I am now eye to eye with his muscular chest, so I bring my gaze up to meet his.

"I would love to take you out to dinner. You know, to really thank you for your time," he says with a sexy grin.

I gulp. I really want to say yes, but I know it won't end well. Before I can get my answer out, the door to the lab opens, revealing Sawyer on the other side. The soldier and I step away from each other. He turns and salutes his captain.

"At ease, soldier," Sawyer commands, and the soldier puts his hand down. "You are dismissed. I need to have a word with Miss Cosimo."

Without a word, the soldier leaves the room. Once the door is closed, Sawyer turns his hard gaze on me. "Why are you here?" he asks.

"Campbell called me in to service some of his men's prosthetics," I answer, trying my best to keep my composure. I'm still pissed at Sawyer but he looks so damn good in his uniform.

"He called you?" he asks, sounding surprised.

I roll my eyes. "Eli was out of town when he called. I asked Eli if he wanted to come, but he said he was too important for house calls."

"So Campbell's not trying to recruit you for his special project?"

I was silly to think that his anger on coming in here was jealousy and not outrage that I lied to him about whatever the hell Campbell was up to.

"Not that I know of," I answer, folding my arms in front of me. I am completely over this conversation.

He moves closer to me, forcing me to look up to face him. His lips are almost distractingly close to mine. "You would tell me if he was, right?"

I exhale heavily through my nose to free myself of the distraction that was his intoxicating scent. "Yes, I would."

I'm not entirely sure if that's the truth. This was exactly our problem. He would act like we had this deep connection when it suited him, but when I spoke about anything remotely close to a relationship, he denied it. Staying away from him was the best thing, but it's harder than I'd care to admit. Because if I didn't love him, the mixed signals wouldn't hurt this much.

I lean in, about an inch away from making another mistake, when the sound of someone clearing their throat catches both of our attention.

"You really can't keep it in your pants for one day," Soup says. The comment clearly directed toward me. He didn't say things like that to the men around here.

"He came on to me. I was just about to turn him down when you walked in," I explain, turning away from Sawyer to start packing up the tools I brought.

"Sure you were," Soup mocks before addressing Sawyer. "Don't you have somewhere else to be, Captain?"

"Yes, sir," Sawyer replies before heading out of the room.

"You know I came here as a favour to you," I say to Soup once we are alone.

He stands in his best intimidating pose, arms crossed, all muscles and height. He's also in his uniform but had his usual hat on over his bald head. His looming presence doesn't affect me, I know what's underneath, just a small little man propping himself up on other's success.

"And your former captain just happened to wander in here?" he says accusingly.

"Yes, he did. Why do you care so much?" I ask.

"Who said I care? He's an adult. He can make whatever ill-advised decision he wants to."

I yank the tool box off the table. I'm ready to leave. I try to brush past Soup, but he grabs my arm to stop me.

"I'm sorry," he says. "That was a low blow. Thanks for coming down here. I forget sometimes that you are almost as good at this stuff as Eli is."

"I'm just as good at this stuff as Eli is." I reply.

Something isn't right. Soup never said thank you, not even to Eli. He wants something, and I have a feeling I know exactly what it is.

"Can we talk in my office?" he asks.

I nod, and he heads out of the small lab, fully expecting me to follow him. As we walk to his office, I try to come up with the best way to use this to my advantage. If Soup is coming to me, he must be desperate. Luckily, I have something I need from him as well.

Soup's office is in one of the hangars, the large doors are open, letting a warm breeze into the warehouse-like space. Soldiers are milling about doing their tasks. They are all in uniform which makes me stand out like a sore thumb in my crop t-shirt and leggings. I get a few looks and whispers as my reputation usually precedes me in this place—mind you, how great my ass looks in these leggings doesn't help.

Soup leads me through the glass door to the briefing room outside of his office. A few guys from his special ops team are in there. One of them has a big scar across his eye, I forget his name but he's always staring at me. I glance his way, and he winks and licks his lips. I roll my eyes and continue to follow Soup into his office.

The decor style for Soup's office is 'powerful man works here.' All wooden, with a giant desk in the middle of the room, a big leather chair sits behind it and two small chairs sit in front of it. The goal of the furniture choices is obviously to make others feel inadequate, but for me it's like watching a magic show when you can see the strings. I could see right through it, so it no longer has any power over me. This wasn't a room I'm comfortable in; in fact, it was home to a lot of bad memories, but I'm not the scared girl who first walked in here at six years old anymore.

I sit in the chair meant for guests and rest my feet on the desk. I track Soup with my eyes as he sits behind his desk. His typical move was to push my feet back to the floor, but he doesn't today. I guess he really wants to stay on my good side.

"So, what can I do for you, Soupy?" I ask.

"Well, as you know, part of the Cosimo Tech contract requires you to create a piece of proprietary technology for us," Soup explains condescendingly. *He is off to a really great start.*

"The contract requires Eli to provide you with that technology," I clarify.

"Yes, well, Eli is going through a hard time right now, isn't he? Maybe you should see this as your chance to take more of a leadership role in the company. Finally do something your father can be proud of."

I keep the confident smirk on my face to mask that he struck a nerve. "Why don't you just cut the charade and tell me what it is you want from me."

Soup's eye twitches slightly, the only tell that I have wormed my way under his skin. "I have been working on a project and I've hit a bit of a wall. I could use a fresh pair of eyes on it."

"What kind of project?" I ask, taking my feet off his desk, leaning forward, not sure if I am feigning interest or actually interested.

"Well, it isn't dissimilar to Eli's prosthetics, only I want to find a way to enhance the entire soldier, not just a missing limb," he explains, like invoking what Eli did for amputees will somehow make his idea sound ethical.

"Like replacing them with robots?"

"No, a bio-enhancement of some kind," he clarifies.

"That you have been testing on human subjects?"

From what Sawyer told me, the answer is probably yes, but I am curious if Soup will admit to it.

"I'm afraid I can't divulge any more information until you're officially on the project and have been given the proper clearance."

I guess that means I'm right.

"I'll think about it." There's no way I would help him with this, but Soup doesn't know that yet. "If you are looking for ways to convince me. I could perhaps be swayed closer to your side with a few goats from your parents' farm."

"Goats?" he asks.

"Goats," I repeat.

"Fine. I'll see what I can do." He waves me out of the room. He has hit his capacity for my shenanigans today.

I stand and start to head towards the door when he stops me. "Ace, what I just told you is highly confidential. You can't tell anyone, not even your little boyfriend. I'm not an idiot, I know he's been poking around."

"He's not my boyfriend."

"It didn't look like that back in the lab."

"Yeah, well, you should ask him then. He'll tell you very clearly that he's not."

I have hit my capacity for assholes today, so I storm out of the room, slamming the door behind me.

CHAPTER 5

Goats may be the single most annoying animals on the face of the planet. I swear, they have not stopped making noise for a single second since Soup delivered them here two days ago. He asked again what we needed them for and I told him we were going to keep them as pets to keep the lawn under control. A way to save the burning of fossil fuels by the lawn mower. I don't know if he bought it, but I also didn't care.

"Are you ready for an adventure?" I ask the

little brown goat. I named him Gerald. Eli said I shouldn't name the goats because if something goes wrong with our tests, I'll be too attached. But it felt wrong to let the little guy head into the unknown without a name.

"Can you stop talking to the damn goat and just put it into position," Eli yells from his post behind the holographic screen of the closest lab table.

I give Gerald a pat on his head and put his little rope leash around his neck. I use a piece of hay to guide him out of the little makeshift pen we made in the corner of the room and onto the round platform of the time machine.

I leave a little pile of hay where we need him to stand and slowly back away, making sure he doesn't move.

"We're sure he is going to be alright?" I ask Eli as I move to stand next to him.

"Yes. All the machine is going to do is use concentrated rays of light to change the frequency of the subject's cells and allow it to move through time," Eli explains.

"So you are moving an object through time by shining a big flashlight on it?" I ask, still not quite believing that this was how we were going to achieve time travel.

"Your brain makes your arm move by sending an electrical signal. Nothing makes sense," Eli answers.

I'm not about to argue with him about the nonsensical nature of science, so I stop the argument there. For the sake of my sanity, I was hoping the test would fail, but not in a way that would hurt Gerald. Maybe I was getting attached to the stupid, annoying thing.

"Subject is in position?" Eli starts his checks.

"His name is Gerald." Eli glares at me. "Check."

"Date and time are correctly entered in the control panel?" he asks.

"Check. Why the hell are you sending him to 1945, anyway? Shouldn't we try something closer?"

Eli hadn't let me in on all the details of the test until today. The glare he gave me is an indication of why. He usually waited to tell me things until it was too late to do anything about my questions.

"Because the farther away we send him, the less likely he is to alter the timeline." Eli explains.

"You're worried that Gerald is going to run into his past self?"

He answers me with a third glare, and definitely not the last for today. "It's just that 1945 seems so random," I push.

It's unlike Eli to be so arbitrary with things. He typically put a lot of thought into the smallest details.

"I calculated it would be best. Can we move forward with the test now?" So far, my help had only consisted of reading through Eli's research and double checking his equations. I didn't recall any about finding a test date but there were so many to go through that maybe I forgot. Everything seemed sound in theory but if I have learned anything in my years working in science, it's that theory doesn't always translate to the real world.

Eli pushes a few more buttons and the time machine whirs to life. "Three…two…one…"Eli counts down and then hits one last button. An almost blinding flare of light emits from the arms of the machine enveloping the goat, and when they dim, Gerald is gone.

Eli does a small fist bump in victory, but the test isn't over yet. We still have to bring him back.

Eli turns a dial on the control pad and hits another button. The time machine whirs again, but this time, the lights don't come on. The whirring goes faster, followed by a loud clang and then silence. No sign of Gerald on the platform.

I look at Eli, trying to hide my relief that it didn't work and my worry for Gerald. "It didn't bring him back."

"No, the machine brought it back, just not to the platform." He starts frantically typing. "If I can get a lock on the frequency, I can find it."

"Find *him*," I correct Eli, but he's not paying attention.

He keeps frantically typing and then lets out a loud "There!" A map appears on the screen with a little red blinking dot that Eli is pointing at. The spot is a few blocks away in an alley.

I pull the handheld monitor out of the drawer and sync it up to the map. Eli and I quickly run up the stairs and make a beeline for the garage. Eli is a car guy, so there are five high-end vehicles to choose from. I run for the one closest to us while Eli goes to the Range Rover.

"Where are you going?" I ask him.

"I am not putting a goat in the Porsche," he answers. I look down at the red sports car and note its lack of back seat.

"Fair point." I go to the Range Rover and slide into the passenger seat as Eli opens the garage door.

I use the handheld screen to guide Eli through the streets until we get deeper into the city. The dot that signifies Gerald isn't moving, which feels weird for a goat. We park the car as close as we can to the alley where the signal is coming from. We run down the street, past small shops and restaurants. It is late in the evening so the street isn't busy with foot traffic but there are a lot of cars out and about. We round the corner between a little bookstore and a hipster coffee bar, expecting to see Gerald safe and sound.

But Gerald isn't in the alley.

Standing next to a large dumpster where the device said Gerald is supposed to be is a man.

CHAPTER 6

Eli and I stop in our tracks, staring at the man at the other end of the alley. I look down at the map again. I zoom in as far as I can and double check that on the other end of the dumpster—in the spot where a very confused-looking man is now standing—there was supposed to be a goat.

"Gerald?" I ask, taking a shot in the dark.

"You think that's Gerald?" Eli questions, as if I had said the most ridiculous thing in the world.

"We just sent a goat back in time using beams

of light. That goat turning into a human would be the least weird thing to happen today," I argue.

"I'm not a goat," the man says. *I guess we were louder than I thought.* "My name is Steve."

Steve looks nervous. He also looks hot. He has sandy brown hair and blue eyes, a very clean cut, wholesome look. That usually isn't my type, but when it's paired with a white t-shirt that can barely contain his muscular arms, I'm willing to be a corrupting influence.

I can't think about him like that, though. It's very likely we just brought this man to the future. The last thing he needs is me flirting with him.

I take a settling breath and put on my most reassuring smile. "Hi, Steve, this is probably going to sound like a weird question, but what year do you think it is?" I ask him, keeping my voice gentle.

"Well, when I woke up this morning, it was 1945. But that thing you are holding and the cars on the street are making me think that it's not 1945," he answers.

"Well, you have great observational skills, Steve. Can you give us a sec?" Eli says while grabbing my arm and pulling me away from Steve, closer to the street. "What the hell are we going to do about that?" he whisper-yells at me.

"*That* is a human being. One that we are now responsible for," I answer, trying to keep a calm expression so as to not freak out Steve any more than he already is. Eli certainly isn't helping in that department.

"What do you mean, *he's our responsibility*?"

I'm not surprised by his reaction. Eli's allergic to responsibility.

"I mean, we plucked him out of his normal life in 1945. So, we have to figure out how that happened and how to put him back," I explain sternly, still whispering as to not alarm Steve.

"So, we have to take him home?" Eli asks, glancing over at the man in question.

"Yes. Where else would we take him?" I say, completely exasperated.

"We could just…" Eli trails off, noticing the disapproval on my face.

"You aren't seriously suggesting we leave him here."

"Fine, you're right. So, which one of us should talk to him?"

"Well, obviously, it should be me," I say.

"Why obviously you?" Eli says, offended.

"Because you're an asshole." That comment earns me the fourth Eli glare of the day. "I'm sorry. Did you want to go talk to him?" I ask, knowing full well the answer is no.

"It would have been nice to at least be considered as an option," Eli says with a huff. "I'll go get the car."

Eli heads down the street, leaving me alone with Steve. I walk around the dumpster that took up a lot of the space between the two small shops. Steve is sitting on a wooden crate, his foot bouncing on the ground, muttering to himself.

"Hi, again. My name is Ace." I step a little closer to him and he looks up. My eyes are drawn to his. Even though he's probably freaking out, his blue eyes have a warmth to them, a sense of comfort.

I kneel to get on his level. "Look, I know that this is probably really scary and overwhelming for you. But if you come with us, I promise I'll help you get home."

His foot stops tapping at the mention of home. His expression is serious as I watch him scan my face. No doubt trying to determine what my motives are.

"I know you have no reason to trust me, but you are currently sitting in an alley next to a dumpster. You don't really have a lot of options," I say.

"Okay," he says quietly.

We stand, and he quietly follows me to where Eli was waiting with the car.

We ride back to the house in silence. I sneak casual glances at Steve through the rear-view mirror. He is taking in his surroundings with a quiet precision. I recognize it immediately as a military reflex, noting escape routes and landmarks. He must have been a soldier of some kind back in 1945.

As we pull up to Eli's Malibu mansion, I can see the stoic expression on Steve's face turn into one of awe. I can't blame him. I still can't believe I live in this modern monstrosity. It was built into the cliff side, looking out on the ocean. A white sleek monument to the futuristic ideals of its owner. I had to talk Eli out of commissioning a giant statue of himself for the front yard on multiple occasions.

We enter the house through the garage. As we step into the foyer, Steve turns around, taking in all 360 degrees of the circular room. His eyes scan the curved staircase that leads to the second floor and then follow the chandelier made up of glass balls that spiral all the way down to the floor.

Joy is waiting for us at the base of the stairs. Eli must have texted her, and judging by the thinly veiled scowl on her face, she isn't exactly happy about him taking in another stray.

"Steve, this is Joy. She can show you the guest room," I say, gesturing to the housekeeper. I step closer to Steve and put a comforting hand on his arm. "There's a shower up there and I can bring you something to sleep in."

"That would be very nice. Thank you, Miss…" He trails off, not knowing my last name.

"Cosimo. But please just call me Ace." I smile up at him.

"Thank you, Ace," he says. He shoots me a small smile back as he walks past to follow Joy, and I swear my heart stops. This man is dangerously beautiful. I shake off my attraction. My focus needs to be on getting him back to his time, not on how unbelievably good his ass looks going up the stairs.

I look away from him for the sake of my sanity and turn to Eli, who has his arms crossed in front of him. A disappointed look on his face like I'm a misbehaving toddler.

"Are you done ogling our guest?" he asks.

"I was not ogling him. I was checking him for any signs of what brought him here," I lie, unconvincingly.

"Sure you were."

I ignore Eli's comment and start the discussion we need to have. "So, what do we do now?" I ask.

"You are the one that wanted to bring him here. What do you think we should do now?" Eli throws the ball back into my court. This is how we operate. He fucks up, and it's my job to fix it.

"You are the one that built the time machine," I argue.

"Maybe we should stick him back in it. Just send him back," Eli suggests.

"We can't do that. Gerald is still missing. We don't know if it's safe to put a person in there," I point out.

"We may not know what happened to Gerald, but Steve here, is fit as a fiddle. He'll probably be fine if we send him back."

"We don't know that. What if something is wrong with him internally? We should get him checked out by a doctor." There is no way I'm going to let Eli use Steve as a lab rat. We have no idea what the implications would be on the timeline if we kept him here, but we also have no idea what moving through time actually did to him.

"Please, you have checked him out enough. Besides, what are we going to tell the doctor? Hey doc, can you check out this man from the past?" Eli asks in his most condescending tone.

"I can text Natalie. We can make up some kind of story about finding him somewhere," I suggest, but I know I'm not going to get Eli on board with any plan I come up with unless there is something in it for him. "He's our most valuable asset in getting the time machine up and running. If we figure out why he was brought here instead of Gerald, we can keep the mistake from happening again."

Eli is uncharacteristically quiet as he

contemplates my proposal. He crinkles his nose the way he always does when I am right, like his body rejects the fact that I could be smarter than him. "Fine. Get Natalie here first thing tomorrow morning."

Eli starts to walk toward the kitchen where the door to the lab was located. "Where are you going?" I ask him.

"To get a snack," he answers. Then, mumbling under his breath, he adds, "Then maybe make some adjustments to the time machine."

"What kind of adjustments?"

"Oh, you know, tighten a screw here, push a button there." He's still mumbling.

"So you know what went wrong, then?"

"Well, I won't know unless I look at the machine."

"Fine, but no more tests until we figure out how Steve got here."

Eli's response is to roll his eyes at me before making his way back to the lab.

I pull my phone out to text Natalie as I head up the stairs to find Steve something to wear.

CHAPTER 7

I clutch a pair of pyjama pants I found in my closet as I stand outside the guest room door. They were Sawyer's. The fact that he kept pyjamas here and yet expected me to believe we weren't in a full-blown relationship was just one of the many mixed signals he had thrown at me. I shake the thoughts of Sawyer out of my head before I knock on the door.

The door opens, and I realize what a spectacular mistake I have made. Steve has just gotten out of the shower. He's now standing in front of me with a towel wrapped around his waist and his six-pack abs glistening in the light. That is all I let myself notice before bringing my eyes back to his face.

"I brought you pyjamas," I say, once my brain can form words.

"Thank you," he says as he takes the pants from me.

"Joy usually does laundry overnight. I don't know why. I have this theory that she's nocturnal." I keep the rest of my vampire theory to myself, no need to scare him any more. "If you give me your clothes, I can throw them down the laundry chute."

"Let me just go get them," he says. I watch as he heads to the dresser where he'd neatly folded the t-shirt and khakis he had been wearing. It gives me a nice view of his damp back muscles, which were somehow even hotter than the front ones.

He hands me the pile of clothes. "I'll get rid of these and come right back. Give you a chance to get changed," I say.

He nods, and goes into the ensuite bathroom as I turn to leave.

I use the walk to the laundry chute to tell

myself that it is a very bad idea to be attracted to him. He needs to go back to his own time. I take it slow heading back to the room, mentally preparing myself to stay on topic when I get back in there.

I stop and look into the open door to see Steve sitting on the bed with his head in his hands, muttering to himself. I take him in for a minute and it gives me a bit more resolve. He's been through a lot today. The best thing I can do for him is to treat him like a person. I knock softly, trying not to startle him.

He looks up at me with those blue eyes of his. It doesn't look like he has been crying, but his brow is furrowed like he's been deep in thought.

"Can I come in?" I ask, not wanting to intrude on his alone time.

"Of course," he answers, moving over on the bed

I sit down next to him and searched for the words to say in this situation. There isn't really a *sorry we pulled you eighty years into the future* card.

"Can you explain to me what happened?" Steve asks. He looks at me, waiting for an answer.

My instinct when talking to someone new,

especially a man, is to gauge exactly how much I could reveal. Something about Steve makes me want to tell him the whole truth, and that isn't something I can usually do. However, in this situation, maybe I can. Who is he going to tell?

"My father, Eli, invented a time machine, and we tested it today. We tried to bring our test subject back from where we sent it and instead brought back you."

"So, the man that was with you was your father?"

"Yes, but nobody knows he's my father. So, don't tell anyone," I warn him.

"No one knows?" Steve looks perplexed by the notion, and I can't blame him. The entire situation is ridiculous.

"He's this hot shot tech mogul," I start to explain, but the look of confusion on Steve's face makes me re-evaluate my words. I guess tech mogul wasn't really a thing in 1945. "He's a famous inventor. When he found out he had a kid, he was worried it would ruin his image."

"How would having a child ruin his image?" he asks.

"I'm not sure." I do know, but I'm caught off guard. His question makes me realize that I've never actually told anyone Eli is my father. Everyone that knows has always known. It felt kind of freeing to tell someone. "I was only six at the time. I didn't really understand what was going on." It almost feels wrong to have Steve's sympathy directed at me with what he went through today, so I swiftly change the subject. "How are you holding up?"

"I really need to get home," he replies.

"Do you have someone you need to get back to?"

"Yes, I do."

I try to hide the disappointment I feel. He's off-limits. I shouldn't feel bad that he's in love with someone else, that he has someone waiting for him.

"We are still working out some of the kinks. That's why you're here and not Gerald. At least you aren't a goat. That would have been harder to fix."

Steve smiles briefly, and suddenly, I want to do everything in my power to make him do it again. Something about it makes me feel lighter. He has one of those contagious smiles. You can't help but smile, too.

"Do you remember what you were doing right before you ended up here? It might help us figure out why you were brought here," I ask.

Steve breaks eye contact, looking at the floor. "Yeah, I don't really remember. I know my name is Steve Knight. I remember that it was January 1945. But I can't remember any specific details from the day."

"Well, remembering basic details is a good sign. My friend Natalie is a doctor. She's going to come over in the morning and make sure nothing is medically wrong, if that's okay with you?"

"Having a doctor look me over would actually offer me some peace of mind. Thank you." He finally tears his eyes away from the floor and we lock eyes for what feels like the hundredth time since we found him. It's my turn to look away from him. I stand up from the bed. I need to get out of here before I do something I regret.

"So, what year is it exactly?" he asks.

"2024," I answer. He takes a deep breath in.

"What have I missed? Have the Brooklyn Dodgers won the World Series?"

"I have no idea, but they did move to Los

Angeles. Maybe we could go to a game."

"That would be nice, but I don't think I can stay here that long."

Right. He has someone to get back to.

"I should let you get some sleep." I turn to leave, but he gently grabs my hand. I look at our joined hands, then at his face.

"Can you stay?" I recognize the shade of fear in his eyes. This isn't him coming on to me. He doesn't want to be alone.

"Sure," I answer. I don't want to be alone, either.

Lying next to Steve in the dark, I am suddenly very aware of how little I am wearing. It's my typical pyjamas, an oversized t-shirt and little shorts, but in this moment, it just adds to the awkwardness.

We are facing opposite directions, and I find myself wondering if Steve has fallen asleep. Maybe if he has, I can sneak out.

The answer to my question comes when I feel him turn over. "I know this is childish. I'm a grown man. I should be able to sleep by myself," he says.

I shift, so I am facing him. "It's okay," I reassure him.

"Between the army barracks, and sharing a room with my friend Ollie growing up, I honestly can't remember the last time I slept in a room alone. It's too quiet, it feels strange," he explains.

I had mentioned my fear of sleeping alone to Sawyer once. He thought it made me clingy. I really shouldn't be comparing Steve to an ex, but I have never had someone understand this part of me before. "I get it. When I was young, before I lived with my dad, my mom and I shared a bed. She didn't have a lot of money and didn't want to go to Eli for anything, so we shared. It took me a while after she died to get used to sleeping alone. I guess I'm still not totally used to it."

"Any advice on how to adjust?" he asks.

"Whenever I couldn't sleep, my mom and I would watch the clock and when it struck twelve, she would say it's midnight, you've made it to tomorrow, there's nothing else to worry about." I grab my phone off the nightstand. I check the time and it's getting close to midnight.

"What is that thing?" he asks.

"It's a phone."

"Where are the cords? Why does it have a screen? Where do you talk into it?"

I smile and shake my head. "All we need it for now is to tell time."

"You tell time on the phone?"

I nod, and move closer to Steve so that he can see. I haven't been this close to him before. He smells so good, just clean. The light from the phone screen illuminates his face. I take the opportunity to really look at him. His eyelashes are the longest I've seen on a man; his sharp jaw tightens as he watches the time. This is dangerous. I shift my focus back to the changing numbers.

This is another piece of me I have never really shared with anyone. It should feel weird and vulnerable, but it doesn't. Something about Steve has me completely at ease. It could be the fact that I'm the only person he knows, so there is no danger of him sharing it with anyone else, but it feels like more than that.

The time switches from 11:59 to 12:00. "It's midnight. You made it to tomorrow. There is nothing else to worry about," I whisper to him.

My eyes find his blue ones, and we are silent for a long time. I have the urge to lean in to kiss him, but stop myself. It could be my eyes playing tricks on me, but I swear his head pulls back, too.

"I guess…since I have nothing to worry about, you can go back to your room now," he says.

I pull the covers up to my chin. "Nope, I'm comfy now. You're stuck with me," I inform him. I turn over and snuggle into the plush mattress.

I hear a faint chuckle as I close my eyes and fall asleep.

CHAPTER 8

I open my eyes, a little confused as to where I am and exactly whose chest my head is resting on. I turn and find a pair of blue eyes looking back at me.

I quickly sit up, extricating myself from Steve's warm, muscular body. "I'm so sorry," I say, getting out of the bed trying to get farther away from this awkward situation.

"Don't apologize. It was kind of nice," he says with a small smile.

Is he flirting with me? I need to shut this down.

"Natalie will be here soon. I should go get dressed." I turn and head to the door. I stop before putting my hand on the knob and whip back around. "Listen, when you are talking to Natalie, don't tell her about the time machine."

"I thought she was going to help us find out what brought me here?"

"She is. She just doesn't know it," I answer. Steve furrows his brow at me in stern confusion. "We can't risk a lot of people knowing about the time machine."

His face softens. "What would happen if people found out about the time machine?"

"It's dangerous. We don't know what the implications are of you being here and not in your own time. If someone with bad intentions finds it, the results could be catastrophic."

"What are your intentions?" he asks. It's not an accusatory question, he genuinely wants to know.

"I don't have any. I'm just helping Eli."

He nods thoughtfully. "And Eli's intentions?"

"It may be hard to believe, but they are good. A little misguided, but good."

Eli always seemed to have good intentions. His

projects were always geared toward helping others. The only person he didn't seem to have good intentions with was me. I give Steve a small smile and he returns it. Our eyes lock and my heart flutters. I give myself one more breath to just look at him before changing the subject.

"Speaking of Eli, Natalie doesn't know he's my father. So, don't mention that either."

"I thought she was your friend? She doesn't know about your father?" he asks.

"I don't really tell people. We don't want it to get out, so it's safer not to tell anyone," I explain.

"You told me." That damn smile of his shows up again and lights his entire face. I can't keep my lips from turning upward at the sight of it.

I still can't pinpoint exactly what it is that made me tell Steve. The logical part of my brain thinks it's because he's going back to his own time and won't tell anyone. The romantic part thinks it's because we have a connection. "You seem trustworthy." I shrug and pull my eyes away from his before I say anything stupid. Reminding myself that he has someone to go home to. "I'll meet you downstairs."

I leave the room and run right into Joy. She has

Steve's clothes in her hands, neatly folded.

She looks at me and then at the door I just came out of and back to me. "I'm not cleaning those sheets," she informs me, her voice dripping in judgement.

"They don't need cleaning. Nothing happened," I say defensively.

Joy just looks me up and down. With my oversized shirt, you can't see my shorts underneath. "Sure, it didn't," she remarks and walks past me to Steve's door.

It's not worth arguing with her. I just shake my head and go to my room to get dressed for the day.

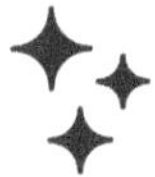

The dining room in the mansion is obnoxiously large, like most things in this house. One wall is floor to ceiling windows that look out on to the ocean, similar to the ones in my bedroom. The walls are painted white and the only furniture in the room is a long antique table that looked like it came out of a medieval castle, and knowing Eli, it probably did.

Steve and I are sitting at one end of the table, waiting for Natalie to arrive. He is fidgeting in his chair, staring at a spot on the table. Joy made us breakfast but he didn't eat very much of it.

"Are you okay?" I ask.

He looks up at me. "Doctors make me nervous," he replies. "Are you sure this is going to help us figure out how to get me back to 1945?"

"Well, we want to make sure it is safe for you. This is the only way to really do that without testing it again," I answer. "We don't want to risk bringing someone else back trying to do another test."

His eyes widen at my response. He turns his focus back to his hands on the table, tapping anxiously.

"I know this is scary. Even though you remember most things about your past, it is still a little worrying that you can't recall specifics about yesterday. Natalie is a neurologist, and if anything is wrong, she'll figure it out." Before I can think better of it, I reach out and take his hand. He stills, and his gaze finds its way back to me. It probably should be awkward, but it's not. I lose track of how long we have been sitting in comfortable silence holding hands when we are interrupted by the arrival of Natalie.

Steve and I drop each other's hands, and he stands. If she saw it, I would never hear the end of it.

"Hi, Nat," I say as she arrives at our end of the table.

"Hi, Ace. I guess this is the patient," she replies, gesturing to Steve.

He reaches out for a handshake. "Steve Knight. Pleased to meet you doctor."

"Nice to meet you, too." She looks him up and down and it causes a pit in my stomach. I've seen her flirt with so many guys, even ones I was interested in and it's never bothered me before.

I decide the best thing to do is get out of there. I tell them I want to give Steve some privacy for this and head down to the lab to check on Eli.

He's sitting at one of the tables staring at the holographic screen in front of him. He's wearing the same ridiculous outfit he's been wearing for the past two days.

"When was the last time you slept or took a shower?" I ask him.

He doesn't look away from the screen. "Not

that long ago. I took a nap on Monday."

"It's Thursday."

"I can't sleep. Look at this. There is no reason that the stupid little goat wasn't the one that came back."

The other goat bleats from his pen in the corner as if to protest the insult to his friend.

"His name is Gerald," I translate, as I lean over to look at the code. Eli's right. The machine is calibrated to locate the specific frequency that it uses to move people through time. "Maybe the frequency changes back too quickly."

"That would explain why the g..." Eli starts, but changes his mind on seeing me glare at him. "Gerald didn't come back. It wouldn't explain why Steve is here."

"Maybe Natalie's check up will give us some answers."

"Or we can bring him down here for some tests," Eli says with a devilish smile.

"No." I usually try to be agreeable with Eli, but I'm not about to let this happen.

"I wasn't asking for your permission."

"I'm not going to let you rope another human

person into your obsession. You're going to end up locking him down here with you for days on end."

Eli stands up and takes a sip from his World's Smartest Man mug. He is taller than me and isn't afraid to use that to intimidate. "I'm sure he's anxious to get home. Unless you want him to stay for some reason, but that would be irresponsible, right?"

I don't respond. I keep my resolve facing him. I can't let him know that he's right. There is a little part of me that wants Steve to stay, but that's not why I want to keep him out of the lab. As much as Eli uses his mind to help people, he's not acting like himself. He isn't taking care of himself. There is a very real chance that he turns Steve into a lab rat to be his means to an end. I can't let him do it.

"Fine. You go take a shower because you stink, and I will bring him to you after he's done with Natalie," I say.

Eli sniffs his armpit and makes a face. "Fine." He puts his mug down and heads up the stairs, and I follow. He heads off to his room and I go back to the dining room. I need to get Steve out of here. If I can buy us some time, then maybe I can talk some sense into Eli.

I get there just as Nat is packing up. "How did it go?" I ask.

"For a man who was mysteriously found near your house, he has a clean bill of health," she says.

I probably could have come up with a better reason as to why he's here. Finding him in an alley and taking him home made him sound like a stray cat.

"So, there is nothing physically wrong with him?" I ask.

"There were a few peculiarities with some of his tests, but nothing to be concerned about," she confirms.

"Peculiarities?" Steve asks.

What did she find? Was it something to do with how he ended up here?

"When we were testing your reflexes they were a little faster than normal but that is nothing to be concerned about," she explains and then turns to me. "Walk me out?"

I nod and pick up one of her bags for her. As we go towards the front door she whispers to me. "You are clear to fuck him if you want."

I slap her arm. "Natalie, it's not like that."

She takes another glance at Steve over her shoulder. "He's hot for a homeless man. I wouldn't judge you."

"He's not homeless," I clarify.

"Then why did you take him in?" she asks.

"Eli tends to take in strays sometimes. How do you think I got here?" Joy always refers to me as the stray that Eli brought home, even though she knew what our real relationship was.

"So, this guy is your long-lost cousin?" Natalie asks.

"No." I didn't need that rumour floating around. I'm not planning on hooking up with Steve, but letting Natalie believe we were related feels like taking the option completely off the table, and I'm not sure I want to do that. "Like I said, we found him."

"Whatever," she says, throwing her supply bag over her shoulder before she leans in and whispers to me. "If you do have sex with him, I want every detail."

I shake my head and hand over her other bag before pushing her gently out the door. "Thank you, Natalie. Goodbye."

She takes the hint and starts walking down the driveway. I watch her to make sure she actually leaves. Before she gets too far, she turns back to me and starts hip thrusting into the air and spanking an invisible ass in front of her. I just flip her off. She gives me one last wave before getting in her car.

I close the door and head back to Steve. "Well, at least we know the time machine didn't affect your health," I tell him.

"She really didn't find anything?" he asks.

"Nothing wrong. You are perfectly normal." With my confirmation, Steve lets out a breath in relief. He must have been really worried.

"You feel fine, right? You don't feel different in any way?" I ask him. I wouldn't have been as nervous as he was if I hadn't felt something was off.

"I feel great," he answers with a smile that erases every suspicion in my head.

"I was thinking that maybe I could take you shopping today," I say. It's the best excuse I can come up with to get him out of the house.

"Shopping? If Natalie didn't find anything, shouldn't we be doing some other tests to figure out what happened with the time machine?"

"I mean we could, but we don't know how long it will take to figure out how to get you back, and Joy will not be happy if she has to wash your clothes every night." Plus, the thought of the clean cut, muscular man in front of me wearing Eli's gaudy wardrobe makes me shudder.

"I don't have any money."

"We brought you almost eighty years into the future. The least I can do is buy you some clothes," I counter.

"I guess that sounds fair," he says with that damn smile again. I have to get away from it.

"Then let's get out of here." I turn and bee line for the exit.

CHAPTER 9

"I don't know about this," Steve says from inside the dressing room. We are at a small boutique in the trendy area of town. The type of place that had snooty salespeople and so little options, it looks more like an art gallery than a clothing store. It wasn't my first choice, but Steve is still adjusting to modern times. The mall would have been overwhelming.

"It can't be that bad," I say, trying to coax him out. I only gave him a pair of jeans and a button down. "We are the only ones in the store. I promise if you look ridiculous, I won't laugh."

"I'm not really concerned about looking ridiculous. It just feels a little tight. I'm afraid it might be too scandalous." Now, I really want him to come out.

"Well, the style for men is a little more scandalous now than it was where you're from." There is no response from the dressing room. I look down at my outfit, which consists of short denim shorts and a tank top. "It can't be any more scandalous than what I am wearing."

The curtain of the dressing room opens, and Steve walks out. He's not wrong. The jeans are tight, probably too tight, but the way they hug his perfect ass is making me debate whether I should tell him to get a bigger size. I lose track of how long I'm staring before my gaze drifts back up to Steve's face, and I notice he's looking at me expectantly, like he had just asked me something.

"I'm sorry. What were you saying?" I ask.

"Does this look okay?" he repeats, looking at himself in the mirror.

"Yeah, it looks great. Though, if it would make you more comfortable, you can probably go up a size in the pants."

"I would be more comfortable in a size up," he replies quickly.

I chuckle softly, and look for where the jeans are. They're hanging up high on the wall. I look around for the saleswoman to help me get them down, but she's nowhere to be found so I grab the little stepladder from the corner and set it up in front of the display. Steve stands close to the ladder. It does something to my heart having him be so protective.

"So, did your wife or girlfriend pick out your clothes for you back home?" I ask while looking for the size.

"I don't have either of those," he answers.

I turn toward him too quickly in reaction, twisting up my feet and losing my balance. Before I can register what's happening, I find myself being held in two strong arms. My face is a breath away from Steve's. His clean smell and blue eyes are begging me to close the distance between us.

"We don't really need the jeans. I have other pants to try on," he says, breaking me out of my trance. All I can bring myself to do is nod.

Steve puts me back on my feet and heads back into the dressing room. I start browsing a display of belts. He's single. It doesn't matter. It doesn't change anything. He's still off limits. But just because I can't date him doesn't mean I can't get to know him.

I pick a belt and take it over to the dressing room, leaning on the door frame. He opens the curtain and I hold up the belt for him. "Last night, you said you had someone to get back to. Who were you talking about?"

He takes the belt from me. "My best friend, Ollie. He's like a brother to me. We took him in after his mother passed. I've sort of felt responsible for him ever since."

"He's really lucky to have you," I say quietly.

Steve's eyes meet mine. I wonder if he can sense how much I wish I had someone like him in my life when my mom died. We stay quiet for a moment while he slides the belt through the loops of the better fitting jeans.

He clears his throat and turns away from me. "You mentioned last night that your mom wanted nothing to do with Eli. How did you end up with him?" he asks as he exits the dressing room again to inspect his new outfit.

I watch him, careful not to lose myself looking at him again. "They were college sweethearts. She found out she was pregnant right after he left her to pursue his grand scientist dreams. She was content to raise me on her own but then she got really sick. She didn't have any other family, so it was either go to Eli or be put in foster care," I explain.

I can see the sympathy in Steve's eyes in the mirror. As a kid, I spent a lot of time being paraded around as Eli's charity case and didn't quite like people feeling sorry for me. I swiftly change the subject. "What is your dad like?"

"My dad died shortly after I was born," he replies.

"I guess I should be thankful that I have a dad. Having a bad dad is probably better than not having one at all."

"That's not always true," Steve says with an understanding look in his eye.

"I really shouldn't be complaining at all. Especially not to you. You grew up during the Great Depression. You were probably huddled around the fireplace with three other families splitting a can of beans for dinner. And here I am, living in a mansion and whining about how daddy doesn't love me."

Steve catches my gaze in the mirror. "Everyone has their own problems, Ace. At least I was huddled around the fire with people who loved me. Love is a basic human need. I'd imagine that feeling alone would be much worse." His words hit a place deep inside me, one that I rarely showed to anyone, one that I didn't even visit myself.

We stand there looking at each other for a few minutes before I look at the floor to pull myself from the trance he seems to have me in. He needs to go back to his time. I can't get attached. "Those pants look much more comfortable."

"They are."

"We'll get them then." I smile at him as he goes back into the dressing room. He comes out a few moments later, wearing the outfit we had found him in and carrying all the clothes we picked out.

"I really can't let you buy all this for me," he says.

I take the clothes from his arms and walk towards the cash register. "Don't worry. I have Eli's credit card."

As the saleswoman—who miraculously appeared once we were ready to spend money—rings up the clothes, Steve and I stand awkwardly at the counter. I take a moment to study his face. He hasn't shaved, so he's starting to get a bit of scruff on his sharp jaw. Those blue eyes of his are scanning the room. It makes sense that he's still on high alert. All of this is new to him. It can't hurt if I just talk to him some more—just to put his mind at ease and make him a little more comfortable.

"So, your friend Ollie, what's he like?" I ask.

Steve gives me a look like he's a little startled by the question, but there's still a hint of that smile on his lips. "Honestly, you kind of remind me of him," he answers.

"Come on. You barely know me," I say, even though at this point I've told him more about myself than I've ever told anyone else.

"I pride myself on being observant." The smile on his face widens, and it makes me forget the fact that flirting with him is a very bad idea.

"Really? So, what have you observed about me?" I ask, taking a step closer to him and flipping my ponytail over my shoulder.

"You are a bit of a spitfire. You mostly follow the rules and do what you're told, but can be a little reckless when the mood strikes you." He's not wrong, but I'm not about to let him know that.

"Is that what Ollie was like?" I ask.

"Yes, though he was often in the mood to be reckless." The way he says reckless does things to me. My brain is screaming at me that he doesn't belong here, I can't get attached. But my heart is telling me that he does belong here. Maybe it wasn't a random choice in time and date that brought him here. Maybe it was fate.

I take another step closer. "What about you, Steve? Do you like being reckless?" I ask as I run a finger down his chest. Out of the corner of my eye I catch his Adam's apple bob slightly.

I am abruptly reminded that Steve and I are not alone by the sound of the saleswoman clearing her throat, interrupting our conversation. "Your total is $1,037.92," she says. I hand her Eli's credit card.

Steve's eyes go wide. "That is a lot of money."

I just shrug. "It's actually cheaper than I thought it would be."

"Ace, you can buy a house for that," he says to

me in a very serious tone.

"You really can't anymore. Inflation."

Steve looks at me like I just rained on his parade.

The woman unceremoniously tosses the receipt in the bag on the counter and hands the card back to me. She turns and leaves without acknowledging us.

I grab the clothes and take Steve's hand, leading him out of the store. We stand on the sidewalk and I look at him. I can't take him back to the house like this. Not only am I still trying to avoid Eli, but I can't have him thinking he's in for some kind of dystopian future.

"We should do something fun," I say.

"I don't think that is a good idea. We should probably go help Eli fix the"—he looks around, noticing that there are other people on the street—"the you-know-what."

"The you-know-what will still be there later tonight. I just think if you are going to be in the future, you should at least have a little fun."

Steve takes a deep breath. I can practically see the war going on in his head between the obligation he feels to protect his friend and the desire he has to just be a guy. I don't know Steve well, but I am also observant and think I can craft the perfect argument.

"If Ollie were here and knew there was a pretty girl in front of you asking you to go have fun with her, what would he want you to say?" I ask.

"He would kill me for not saying yes."

"Then let's go have some fun."

CHAPTER 10

The expression on Steve's face when we walk into the arcade is priceless. A mix between child-like wonder and being completely horrified. So, no different from the feelings any adult has walking into an arcade.

The warehouse is huge and full of every type of arcade game you can imagine. I leave Steve to take in his surroundings while I go buy some tokens. I come back to a man that looks like he has lost all of his resolve.

"We shouldn't be here. I need to get back home," he says.

"Eli is working on it. He will probably get more done without us in his hair," I reply.

"What is this place?"

"It's called an arcade. Usually these kinds of places are always full of screaming children, however this place is hidden away so it's always kind of dead. I honestly don't know how they stay in business. They might be laundering money."

Steve furrows his brow at me again, but I'm determined to loosen him up a bit.

The mission for today has changed. It is no longer just get Steve away from Eli, it is get Steve to open up. Even though I believe that Eli is slowly losing his mind, what I saw in his data today had me thinking. It isn't a coincidence that Steve is here, and not like in a fate has brought us together way; it's in a there is something he's not telling me way.

"We're going to play some games. Let's do a lap and see if there is anything that catches your eye." I take him by the hand and we start walking around.

As we make our way through the aisles of games, I just watch Steve's face. It's kind of fun to watch him taking it all in.

"That one. Skee-ball. I've played that before," he says, pointing to the machine.

"You have?" He nods at me, and that glorious smile is back on his face. "Good, then I won't have to go easy on you."

I give him a token and tell him how to start it up. We hit the button at the same time and the balls come down the chute. I start rolling balls up the runway like a champ, just trying to get them in any hole. Some might think the best strategy for Skee-ball is to go for the corners because they give you more points, but I find with games like this, the best strategy is no strategy.

In what seems like not nearly enough time, I am out of balls and I look up at the scores. Steve won and tickets are pouring out of his machine. "What are these for?"

"You take them to the counter and you can trade them in for prizes." He nods in understanding, but he has a far off look in his eye. "Everything okay?"

"They had games near the beach when Ollie and I were in high school. We used to take girls there and try to impress them by winning a prize. We weren't very good, so it rarely worked."

"So, are you going to try to impress me by winning me a prize?" I ask. Hoping it doesn't come off as flirty as I intended it. I really need to stop flirting with him, it's bad for both of us.

"Absolutely, I am."

I can't help the smile that has found its way on to my face. "You seem pretty confident, but it's my turn to pick the game now."

I grab Steve by the hand again and take him to my favourite game, Dance Dance Revolution. He sees it and his confidence evaporates. "It's a dancing game?" he asks.

"Don't worry, it's barely dancing. You just stand on the platform and step on the arrow as it comes up on the screen," I explain.

We both get up on the platforms and I take my phone out of my pocket so it doesn't fall. I look at my notifications for the first time since I left the house and see that Eli has tried to call many, many times.

My expression falls and Steve takes notice. "Everything okay?" he asks.

I try my best to bring my mood back up. "Just

a telemarketer."

"What's a telemarketer?"

"Someone who calls you and tries to sell you things."

"How do they get your phone number?"

"That, Steve, is one of life's great mysteries," I answer as I put the tokens in to the game.

I select a good beginner song and we start playing. I can do this song with my hands tied behind my back, so I take the opportunity to watch Steve stumble through. He's not doing terribly, his eyes are narrowed in deep concentration and he's biting his lip. It's so sexy I have to look away.

The song finishes, and I win by a large margin, so the tickets start pouring out of my side of the machine. I grab them and wave them in front of Steve. "Looks like I might be the one winning a prize to impress you," I say smugly.

"You already impress me, Ace," he replies, and I stop breathing.

I regain my composure enough to speak. "Let's go find another game."

I take a step off the platform, but Steve stops me before I can get too far. "Ace, your phone." He looks at the screen as he hands it to me. "Why does it say Eli on it? Is he trying to call you?"

I could lie to him again, but something about that sweet golden retriever face of his makes it impossible. If I expected him to trust me, I had to be honest. "Yes, he's been trying to call all day," I admit.

"You should call him. What if it is about something important?"

I take a deep breath and look down at the floor, hoping he doesn't hate me for what I'm about to say. "I don't have to answer. I already know what he wants. He wants you."

"Why does he want me?"

"This morning he told me about something he found with the time machine. He thinks there is something different about you and he wants to run tests. I know it sounds like nothing but I know Eli—he hyper fixates on these things and once he starts you'll just become a lab rat to him and I can't let that happen. We are going to get you back, I just needed some time to figure out how best to go about it."

Steve is quiet for a moment, before I feel his finger under my chin, tilting my head up to meet his gaze. "So, today hasn't been about clothes or having fun. You were trying to protect me?"

I nod. His face is once again within kissing distance and I want so badly to move that inch forward to feel his perfect lips on mine. "If you want to go back to the house, I'll understand," I say.

My words seem to snap us both out of a trance. He puts his hand down and he takes a step back. "We still have prizes to win," he says with a sexy little grin.

This man is going to be the death of me.

We step away from Dance Dance Revolution to look for another game. "So, what does Eli think is different about me that would affect the time machine?" Steve asks.

"I don't think you would understand even if I explained it to you," I answer, while looking for something fun and easy for Steve to learn.

"It could be worth a try. Maybe something you say will jog my memory."

"Well the time machine changes a person's frequency—or in this case, a goat's—then searches for that frequency at the destination date to bring it back. It seems as though your frequency was picked up by the machine and we just don't know why. You got any ideas?"

Steve avoids eye contact as he answers, "I don't even know what frequency is. I don't know what it could be."

I can't help but think he's not telling the truth. He knows something, he's just not telling me. I'll just have to be even more charming.

Out of the corner of my eye, I spot the perfect game. I grab Steve's hand and drag him over to the punching bag game.

"What game is this?" he asks.

"It tests your strength. You hit the punching bag and then it gives you tickets based on how strong you are," I explain.

"That sounds kind of boring." He puts his hands in his pockets and is shying away a little more than he was before.

"You scared you aren't going to be strong enough?"

"No, that's not it."

"It's designed to be difficult. I won't judge you on the outcome, it's all in the precision of where you hit it, not your actual strength," I reassure him.

"Well, if it isn't an actual measurement of

strength, then I guess it could be fun," he concedes.

"That's the spirit." I take a step back to give him a bit of space.

He winds up and punches the punching bag and it pushes back into the machine. The lights on the meter shine all the way up to the top. Jackpot bells start ringing and more tickets than I have ever seen start pouring out of the machine, and they don't stop.

I turn to Steve and his brows are knitted together in concern. "Is it supposed to do that?"

"I guess you hit it in the precise spot," I reply with a shrug. I guess his muscles aren't just for show.

CHAPTER 11

Steve and I walk through the front door with the spoils of our day on the town. He has the bags from our shopping trip, while I hold the comically large teddy bear we left the arcade with. The owner let us have it as long as we agreed never to come back after breaking the punching game.

"You took him shopping," Eli says through gritted teeth.

"He needed clothes," I reply matter-of-factly.

"Did he also need a teddy bear?"

"If you must know, yes he did."

"What happened to bringing him down to me? Not to mention how stupid it is that you took him out in public. What if someone saw him?"

I've seen Eli angry before, but this is intense. The veins in his forehead are popping out and his entire body is clenched. Plus, half his argument doesn't make sense. Why would it matter if anyone sees Steve?

"If someone saw him, they would think 'hey, there goes a completely normal dude,'" I answer.

"Ace, we built a time machine. People can't know about it. We are supposed to be figuring out how to get him back, not dressing him up like some life size Ken doll. I knew I couldn't trust you to help with this," Eli yells.

No, he's not about to put this back on me. I step closer to Eli and hold myself as tall as I can. "You practically begged me to help you. Because I'm not your obedient little pet, all of a sudden you can't trust me to help anymore," I yell back.

"This isn't about obedience. It's about you not being a complete and total hindrance to the entire process." He lets out a groan and shakes his head, then says to himself. "Why do I let you even live here?"

All the fight I have in me leaves with those words. All these years of trying so hard to impress him and it all falls apart because I tried to do the right thing. I feel myself physically deflate, and Steve must have noticed because he steps forward, taking a protective stance in front of me.

"I can hear you," he says. Eli takes a step back at Steve's stern tone. "I'm a human being, not some part from your time machine you need to fix."

"I know you're a human being. And with all due respect, you have no idea what you are talking—" Eli starts to defend himself, but Steve cuts him off.

"Really? Because the only person who has made me feel like a person and not a science experiment is Ace." Eli is looking at me now, but I don't know what to say. I have never seen anyone stand up to Eli before, especially not on my behalf. "You owe her an apology."

"I, what now?" Eli looks genuinely confused. I don't think I have ever seen him apologize to anyone ever, and if I had to guess who would be the first person to get his apology, it certainly wouldn't be me.

"She was the one who told you to bring me back here. She was the one who had the idea of bringing in a doctor to check me out. If not for her, I would probably be wandering the streets asking people what year it was. Then you would have been in trouble," Steve continues. He has stepped closer to Eli and is towering over him now.

I should be enjoying seeing Eli's methods being used against him, but I can't help but wonder about what Steve said. How does he know those things? We were far away from him, whispering when we talked about bringing him home, and he was a full floor above us when I mentioned bringing in Natalie.

"I'm not apologizing to her. She's the one who went behind my back. There are still tests that need to be done to get you home," Eli argues.

Steve opens his mouth to give his rebuttal, but I put a hand on his arm to stop him. He turns to me, and I mouth, "It's okay."

He nods and brings his focus back to Eli. "Whatever tests you want to do; Ace can do them. I trust her."

"What makes you think you have any say in the

matter?" Eli complains.

Steve puffs out his chest and crosses his arms. He is probably only an inch or two taller, but his presence feels so much larger. "Fine." Eli concedes and turns tail to head up the stairs

I follow and catch him before he gets there. "Why are you worried someone would recognize him?" I ask him.

Eli takes a moment to try to formulate an answer. "You're right," he finally says. "There is no reason anyone should recognize him. It's been a long day. I'm going to bed."

I can't help the feeling that something is off as I watch Eli head up the stairs. It's Steve's voice that finally pulls me out of my head.

"Are you alright?" he asks.

I look up into his blue eyes that still radiate warmth despite the fact he is probably still fuming from the argument. Something about the way he looks at me makes every question and concern leave my brain.

"I'm fine," I answer. "No one has ever stuck up for me like that before."

"Well, I meant what I said. If it wasn't for you,

I would be lost. You made me feel less alone in a place where I don't know anyone," he says.

The funny thing is he's the one that makes me feel less alone. I have never been able to talk to anyone about my real relationship with Eli. Steve is something special, and I am done fighting my feelings.

I drop the teddy bear on the floor and take his face in my hands, pulling him into me, pressing my lips to his in a fiery kiss.

It takes a few seconds to become fully aware of what I've just done. You can't just kiss someone out of nowhere. I pull back as quickly as I launched myself at him.

"I'm so sorry. I shouldn't have done that," I apologize.

Steve looks at me. I can see that his brain is still processing what just happened, but he didn't look upset. I turn away, it feels wrong to look at him.

"It's okay," he says politely.

"No, it isn't. I…" I stop talking as I hear the bags he's holding hit the floor and feel his hand brush against mine. He fully takes it and pulls it gently until I turn to meet his eyes again.

"Ace, it is really okay." That is all the permission I need.

My arms wrap around his neck, and our lips meet again, only this time he kisses me back. I can feel his big strong arms making their way around my waist, pulling me closer to him. I climb the giant bear between us to wrap my legs around his waist.

I reluctantly remove my mouth from his to catch my breath. "Do you feel like being reckless?" I ask him.

"Yes," he answers without hesitation, and kisses me again.

CHAPTER 12

My legs are wrapped around Steve's waist as he carries me into the bedroom, attached at the lips. My tongue is exploring his mouth as he gently lays me on my bed. He pulls away for a moment, looking down at me.

"Are you sure you want to do this?" he asks. There's a fire in his blue eyes, but there also seems to be a hint of fear. A wave of realization washes over me. People were far more conservative in the 1940s. Maybe he's asking me as a way out.

"Yes, very sure. Are you sure you want to?" I ask in my most comforting tone.

"Yes," he answers, kissing me again. His hands slowly make their way toward my breast. Not dragging it out in a teasing way, but tentative, like he's nervous.

"Is this okay?" he asks again. It's really sweet that he's making sure I'm okay, but if he's going to ask every time he touches me, this is going to take all night, and not in a good way.

"I'm going to save us some time. You can do whatever you want as long as you don't stick anything up my butt." I give him my blanket consent, and Steve's eyes grow to the size of saucers. Like the idea of ass play has never once entered his wholesome little mind.

"What would I stick up your butt?" he asks, slightly horrified.

I put my hand on his face to comfort him a bit. "Don't worry about it." He doesn't immediately resume kissing me, so I assume he's still worried. "Listen, I have a question for you. Know that the answer is not going to affect whether I have sex with you. So, please be honest."

"Ace, I would never lie to you."

"Are you a virgin?" I ask.

"No," he answers, and I try to contain the sigh of relief to in my head. "I just haven't been with many girls."

I nod, taking in his response while trying to keep the worry off my face. "What did you do with those girls?"

He blushes, looking like he is trying to figure out the politest way to phrase missionary, but then his face quickly shifts. If an animation of a light bulb going off appeared above his head, I would not have been surprised. "We didn't do much. There is something I know how to do, but I didn't do it with them because it felt a little too depraved."

I quirk up an eyebrow. "And you think I'm depraved enough to like it?" I probably am. Thinking about what his bar is, it's probably something like doggy.

"You were talking about sticking things up your butt," he says with a smile and kisses my neck.

"Fair point," I concede.

"My friend, Ollie taught me this. He was better at getting girls than I was." That statement brings up so many questions in my mind, but they will have to wait. Steve's hands finally find their way to the hem of my shirt and I'm not about to delay this longer with more questions.

I lift off the bed enough for him to slide my shirt off. I picked the perfect day not to wear a bra. Steve pauses for a moment to admire my bare chest, but quickly gets back to work. He starts leaving a trail of soft kisses from my jawline down my neck to my collarbone. The feel of his warm lips on my skin is so deliciously good, but a little voice in the back of my head wonders if he's stalling. That voice, along with every other thought I have, leaves my brain entirely when his tongue grazes my nipple.

I close my eyes as I take in the way he teases it. My fingers find their way into his hair as a small moan escapes my lips. He shifts slightly to give the same treatment to the other breast.

"Fuck, Steve. That feels good but isn't exactly depraved," I say between breathy moans.

Once my nipples are sufficiently stimulated, Steve lifts his head to respond. "I haven't gotten to the depraved part yet."

I will probably never meet Ollie, but he is

already my favourite of Steve's friends.

Steve continues his journey down my body. He trails kisses all the way down to the waistband of my shorts. I lift again as he pulls them down along with my panties. Before I know it, I am lying completely naked in front of him.

I watch his Adam's apple bob as he kneels at the end of the bed, taking in my naked body. His hands run slowly from my ass down to the bottom of my thighs.

My legs are framing his face as I look up at him. A small smile spreads across his kiss-swollen lips as we make eye contact. He holds my gaze as he leans his head down and kisses my thigh. I hitch a breath, and he looks back to the task at hand as his lips meet my thigh again.

I close my eyes and feel him move lower and lower down my thigh until the sensation disappears. I'm about to look up and see where he went, but I don't need to. The answer to my question comes in the form of Steve's tongue gently grazing my clit.

"Oh, fuck." These are the only words I am capable of forming as Steve devours my pussy like a man starved. He alternates between sucking and licking my clit. I can feel that telltale pressure building in my abdomen. As if he can read my mind, he sticks two fingers in my entrance, slowly moving them in and out, deeper and deeper.

"Steve," I scream out his name as the dam bursts and the waves of pleasure wash over me, thankful that my room is soundproof. He keeps pumping his fingers until the orgasm passes. He works his way back up my body, leaving kisses along the way until his lips find mine again.

"How was that?" he asks. Not in a cocky way like most guys, but in a genuine way.

"Amazing," I answer. "Your turn."

I push gently on his shoulder to move him to his back and return the favour, but he doesn't budge. He shakes his head and slips off the bed. I open my mouth to tell him to come back, but then I see why he got up.

He grabs the hem of his shirt and pulls it over his head, revealing himself to me. I've seen him without a shirt before but this time I'm actually allowed to take it all in. He has a body that looks like it was sculpted by an artist. You could teach an anatomy class with his torso, every muscle is so perfectly formed. However, once he drops his pants, I find myself completely distracted from his upper body. His cock is already hard, and it's huge. Not an unmanageable size, but just big enough that it will stretch me out perfectly.

Steve climbs back over me and kisses me again. I pull away, once again becoming impatient. "Fuck me, Steve. Please."

Our lips collide as his hand makes its way down to his shaft. He teases my entrance with the tip and my moan is muffled by our kiss.

He slowly sinks in to me bit by bit. Pulling out a little before going in a little deeper, helping my body adjust to him. He finally plunges into the hilt, and I moan as he starts to methodically thrust. He goes at a slow pace and I can feel the pleasure building, but it's building too slow.

"Harder," I whisper in his ear, and he takes the note, speeding his pace up slightly. Pulling almost all the way out before gliding back in. It's still not enough. It feels mind numbingly good, but he's not going at the pace I need him to. I place my hand on his shoulder and look up at him. "I have an idea. Get on your back."

He scrunches his eyebrows in confusion but follows my instruction. He rolls off of me, lying on his back with his head propped up on the pillows.

I straddle him just above his hips. "You ready?" I ask him.

He nods in excitement. I lift my ass and shift back slightly, slowly impaling myself on his glorious cock. I close my eyes and let out an almost pornographic moan as I bottom out.

I place my hands on his chest and shift until I find the perfect angle, so he's hitting the exact right spot inside of me. I use the leverage to move up and down, and watch Steve's eyes roll back in his head. I go a little faster, finally reaching the pace I have been craving as he braces himself by putting his hand above his head and gripping the headboard.

I pick up speed, my climax approaching like a freight train, and with a shout, I come all over his cock. I can tell from the expression on his face that he's close, too. He uses his grip on the headboard to drive up into me, prolonging my orgasm as he approaches his. I close my eyes and hear his moans as he finally goes over the edge, filling me with his cum.

After a few deep breaths, slowly coming down from my high, I open my eyes.

The sight immediately sobers me. In Steve's hand is a large piece of wood—half of my headboard to be exact.

CHAPTER 13

Steve and I stand at the end of my bed, surveying the damage. We had taken the time to get partially dressed. Steve put his underwear on and I put on his t-shirt. He's still holding half of my headboard.

He's looking at what remains of my bedroom decor. I look at the piece of wood in his hands, then back up at what remains of my bed.

"Steve. What aren't you telling me?" I ask.

"What do you mean?" he replies. He turns to me and there is genuine confusion on his face.

"You broke my headboard," I answer, pointing to the mess that Joy is definitely going to refuse to clean up.

"I'm really sorry about that. I can find a way to pay for it," he apologizes.

I take a breath and adjust my tone. I'm not mad at him, just worried, and a little confused. "No, that's not the problem. The problem is that it is made of Black Ironwood, imported from across the country. It's the hardest wood found in North America and able to withstand over 3000 pounds of force. And it's broken."

Steve turns back to the headboard. He's pursing his lips as he examines the damage, his gaze moving back and forth between the piece of wood in his hand and where it came from.

I put my hand on his, which brings his focus back to me. "It's okay. You can tell me, I say softly.

He takes a deep breath and looks at our joined hands, rather than my face. "Back in 1945, I signed up to be part of an experimental military operation. They sold it to us as special operations, but it was more specialized than we initially thought. When your time machine brought me to the future, they were experimenting on me. The results were supposed to be heightened senses and elevated strength," he explains.

"So, that's how you heard Eli and I." All the dots are starting to connect in my head. My mind quickly shifting to other conversations I had where I thought Steve couldn't hear me. "Does that mean you also heard Natalie and I?"

Steve blushes. "I didn't appreciate her language, but it was a bit of an ego boost having her try to convince you to pursue me romantically. She wasn't far off the mark," he says, his eyes drifting over our half-naked bodies and the state of my bed to prove his point.

"Why didn't you tell me? Or at least tell Natalie when she was checking you out?" I ask. I'm a little hurt that he didn't fully trust me. Though I guess he didn't really have a reason to. He doesn't really know me.

"I was scared that you would try to study me. Try to figure out what they did so you could replicate it. I thought that you may want to keep me here."

I let go of his hand and slip my arms around his waist, pulling myself into him. "I'm not going to turn you into an experiment, but we will probably need to know what they did to you in order to figure out how you got here."

I rest my head on his bare muscular chest, and he kisses the top of my head. "We can talk about that tomorrow. Let's get some sleep."

I turn to look at the bed again. "Maybe we should do that in the guest room." I suggest. He smiles and takes my hand, leading me down the hall.

I have always believed that you can tell whether a man is going to be a long-term fixture in your life by how you feel when you wake up next to them. With most of the guys I picked up in bars, I'm usually annoyed when I wake up and they are still there. But with Steve, it's almost comforting to open my eyes and see him lying there.

I watch him sleep for a little while. It's the most peaceful I've seen him since he's arrived here. Even when we were falling asleep last night, he seemed tense. The morning sun shines on his face and it makes me wish his eyes were open so I could see the way it would make the blue sparkle.

"Are you watching me sleep?" he asks without opening his eyes.

"Maybe," I reply coyly, shifting closer to him.

He wraps his arms around my waist and pulls me into his chest. I tilt my head up and place my hand gently on his cheek, tugging him into a soft kiss. I'm rewarded with a glimpse of those gorgeous eyes of his.

"Good morning," he says, his voice gravelly with sleep.

"Good morning," I reply.

As I look at his almost maddeningly perfect face, it occurs to me just how totally fucked I am. As much as I want to believe that fate brought him to me, the logical part of my brain reminds me that him being here is likely detrimental to the timeline and we have to get him back.

"What's wrong?" Steve asks. The worry must show on my face because he's studying my expression.

"Do you have any regrets about last night?" He had given his enthusiastic consent last night but sometimes things look different in the cold light of day. I also couldn't bring myself to tell him that I didn't want him to go. It's too early for that, we just met two days ago.

He pushes a strand of hair behind my ear. "Not one single one. Why would you think that I did?"

"Well, I know things were a bit more conservative in the 40s. You didn't really jump into bed with someone after only knowing them for twenty-four hours."

"You're right about that. I spent my whole life doing things because I thought they were the right thing to do, the things I was supposed to do. But something about you makes me want to throw caution to the wind and do things because I want to do them." The twinkle in his eye makes me pull him in for a kiss.

"We should probably get out of bed soon," I say, kissing him again and not making a move to actually leave.

"Yeah, probably," Steve replies, equally unmotivated to move.

"We need to figure out what to tell Eli about you." It's the unfortunate reality we will eventually have to deal with.

"What do you think we should tell him?" he asks.

That's a hard question. This revelation makes things make a lot more sense. It's not a coincidence that Steve was brought here when he was being experimented on. The experiment had to have changed his frequency to one that was similar to the one the time machine looked for, and that's likely the key to fixing the issue. However, if the issue gets fixed, then Steve will leave. Unless we tell Eli about Steve's abilities, and Eli gets so distracted by trying to figure how Steve got them, he forgets all about the time machine.

Steve kisses my forehead, pulling me from my train of thought. "I didn't mean for that to be a trick question," he says with a smile that causes a little pang of guilt.

This isn't just about me anymore. I'm not the only one that is going to be affected by it.

"What do you want to tell him?" I ask. At the end of the day, it's not my secret to tell.

"My first instinct is to tell him nothing. However, I feel like that may be counterproductive to getting me home," he replies.

"I know you don't want to become some kind of lab rat, but I wouldn't worry too much about that. Eli is motivated to get the time machine up and running. Telling him about the experiment would be our best bet for getting you home," I say, trying not to sound too disappointed at the idea of him leaving.

"It sounds like telling Eli the truth is our only option."

"I mean…we could just stay in this bed forever. I'm sure I could convince Joy to bring us food. As long as she doesn't have to clean up after us," I joke, trying to lighten the mood. The smile making its way across Steve's face, a signal that I succeeded.

"I need to get back home, Ace. There are people who count on me," he says. I think I see regret in his expression, but it is likely a trick of the mind, showing me what I want to see.

"You know; we could find a way to bring Ollie here. Maybe he can teach you some more things," I say, half kidding, half thinking about the things he taught Steve to do and what other pointers he might give him.

"Actually, I take back my answer from before; I do have one regret. Telling you that Ollie taught me to do…that." I giggle at the fact that Steve is so wholesome he can't say oral sex. "Besides, we don't know what my staying here will do to time in general, let alone what bringing someone else to the future will do."

"I know," I whisper, trying my best to keep the full weight of my feelings out of my voice.

He leans in slightly, resting his forehead against mine. "I'm in a hurry to leave because I have to, not because I want to."

I pull him in for another kiss, this one deeper and more passionate. Sure, having sex with him might have been a mistake. It's going to make it so much harder to let him go. But right now, as my lips tangle with his, and his hands find their way to my ass, I can't find it in me to regret it.

CHAPTER 14

If the fact that I'm wearing Steve's shirt from the day before doesn't make it obvious that we hooked up, then the way we're eating breakfast sure does. We're both sitting at the kitchen island, my feet are in his lap, and he's feeding me strawberries in between bites of pancakes.

Joy keeps making a disgusted noise every time she catches a glimpse of us. I can't really blame her. If I was watching someone else act like we were acting, I would throw up from the sweetness. But now that I'm on the inside, I understand. It feels really good being with Steve. He makes me feel safe in a way I have never experienced before. Despite the strange way he entered my life, he chooses to be with me, and not just because I have a hot body or am good at science. I make him feel like he's not alone.

"You have got to be kidding me," Eli's voice cuts through my happy little breakfast bubble.

"Good morning, Eli," I say. "There was a bit of a development last night." I look to Steve for some reassurance. We know it has to be done, but I want to make sure he hasn't changed his mind. He gives me a small nod.

"Please spare me the details. I already have to bleach my eyeballs after the sight of this," Eli says, gesturing largely at how Steve and I are sitting.

"This is not the development I was referring to. Though I guess it is somewhat related. It did come up because he broke my headboard."

Eli stops pouring his coffee and turns around to look at me. "He broke your Ironwood headboard?" he asks, his usual smirk replaced by a look of concern.

"When the time machine brought him here,

Steve was being experimented on by the military," I explain.

Eli scrunches his eyebrows together and takes a sip of his coffee. "And those experiments resulted in superhuman strength," he says, like he's finishing my sentence rather than asking a question.

"Yes, and heightened senses," I confirm, speaking slowly, examining Eli's face to gauge the meaning behind his reaction.

"Do I want to know how you figured out that one?" he asks.

"He told me," I answer, rolling my eyes.

Eli pours the rest of his coffee and takes a sip. He has a far off look in his eye that I recognize all too well.

"I know what you are thinking," I tell him. "The reason the time machine brought him here likely has something to do with the experiments. I had the same thought."

Eli takes another sip of his coffee, processing. "Yeah, you are probably right," he says, and heads out of the kitchen.

Steve and I look at each other with an unspoken "that was weird" look. I get up and follow

Eli to the foyer.

"Where are you going?" I ask, catching him before he's about to head out the door.

"Out. He wants you to run the tests on him anyway. The last thing I need is to watch you two be all googly eyed at each other while you do it," he answers.

Something is off. Eli never trusts me with anything. I grab him by the arm and lead him through the door, closing it behind me.

I take him with me down the front steps and into the middle of the driveway. I'm not sure how good Steve's hearing is, but he probably can't hear us from all the way inside.

"What the hell, Ace?"

Eli protests as he pulls his arm from my grip.

"There is something you are not telling me," I say sternly, trying not to yell.

"There are a lot of things I don't tell you," he says, and turns to go to the garage.

I run past him, cutting him off. "Eli. Need I remind you again that you are the one who asked for my help with this. I can't help you if you don't tell me everything."

"This has nothing to do with the time machine," he says, trying to get around me, but I move in front of him again.

"Bullshit. You were motivated enough to build the thing in three months, you aren't just going to abandon it. Where are you going?" I ask again.

He tries to get around me one more time, but I don't let him. He lets out an exasperated groan. "I'm going to see Campbell. You happy now?"

I most definitely am not. "Why?" I ask.

"You ask so many questions. You always have. It's kind of annoying. It's why I sent you to boarding school when you were six. The incessant question asking."

I ignore Eli's attempt at deflection and ask again. "Why are you going to see Soup? What does he have to do with any of this?"

"I really thought you were smarter than this, Ace. I said no to Campbell, so I'm assuming you were next on his list to help with his little project," Eli explains.

Then it all starts coming together. Steve is an enhanced soldier—the same thing Soup is trying to make.

"You want to hand over Steve," I say.

"It's the only way to keep Campbell off our backs," Eli says, defending himself. He may have a point, but that doesn't make it the right thing to do. If anyone was going to turn Steve into a lab rat, it would be Lawrence fucking Campbell.

"And what are you going to tell Soup when he asks how exactly you came across an enhanced soldier?" I ask, knowing that Eli had a one track mind and him thinking the time machine was at risk was Steve's only hope.

"He's going to find out about the time machine as soon as he sees Steve. If I go talk to him now, at least I can get out in front of it." That's not the answer I'm expecting.

"What do you mean?" I ask.

Eli smiles smugly in reaction to the confused look on my face. "So, Campbell didn't fully explain to you how his little project came about." I want to smack the shit-eating grin off his face, but I let him continue. "He didn't just decide one day to start this project. He came across a file from the 40s about a discontinued experiment. The files were heavily redacted, but the project was shut down after something happened to the test subject."

That little tidbit of information had about twenty trains of thought leaving the station. The least important but the most glaring of which being if Steve disappearing was in this file that Soup found before we tested the time machine, maybe it's okay that Steve is here.

Eli takes advantage of the distraction he caused and finally moves around me, making his way to the garage. I come back to myself and go after him again.

"Wait. You can't just hand Steve over," I tell him.

He takes a deep breath and runs his hands down his face. "I had an inkling about him when he first showed up here. I should have brought him in then before you got attached."

"He's not a puppy. He's a human being. Frankly, the amount of times I have to remind you of that is concerning," I say. My brain is working a mile a minute, trying to put myself in Eli's shoes and come up with an acceptable solution that keeps Steve away from Soup. "Look, the experiment is what brought Steve here, right? So, it's the key to figuring out what went wrong with the time machine. We also know that whatever they did worked, so it is the solution to whatever the hell Campbell is doing, too."

"Where are you going with this, Ace?" Eli asks.

"We figure out what happened to Steve and send him back with the time machine. We can then use what we learned from Steve to help Soup, getting him off our back, but also not hurting any of his test subjects," I explain.

Eli contemplates my idea for a moment. "But how do we stall Campbell? He's not exactly a patient man."

"We tell him we're busy with the Time Keeper launch," I answer.

Eli moves his head back and forth, weighing the options I laid out for him. "Fine," he says. "Just know if Campbell sees Steve and figures out who he is, I will have no problem handing him over."

"It'll be fine. Soup hardly ever leaves the damn base and there is no reason for me to ever bring Steve there. And Steve would have to do something enhanced to clue him in. He hid it from us pretty well," I say more to myself than to Eli.

"There are pictures of the subject in the file,

Ace."

"So what? You didn't recognize him and you've seen the file."

"True, I've seen the file once. Campbell has been studying the thing for months. He probably won't recognize him." I roll my eyes at Eli's sarcasm, but he's not wrong. "But as long as you are sure you can keep him away, then do whatever you want. Just know that if it comes down to Steve or the time machine, I'm picking the time machine," he concedes, and heads toward the garage.

"Wait, where are you going?" I ask. I just talked him out of seeing Soup.

"I'm going to the office to check on the Time Keeper roll out. With you taking time off to spend with our guest, someone needs to pick up the slack at Cosimo," he says, as if he hasn't been hiding out in the basement working on something else for the last three months. "Plus, I meant what I said about not wanting to see the two of you all over each other." He shudders in disgust, and continues on his way.

I stay standing in the driveway for a minute after Eli drives away. Trying to process what had just happened.

Everything is going to be okay. All I have to do is keep Steve away from Soup and figure out how to get him home.

CHAPTER 15

Once we finished breakfast and got dressed, I set Steve up on a chair in the lab and grab the device we had used to track Gerald. My thought process being that Steve might still be emitting the same frequency that caused the time machine to bring him back instead of Gerald.

I pass the device over him and take note of the readings. There are remnants of the frequency, but it's not as strong as the day we found him. I load the data into the computer and start to set up a program to analyze the two frequencies for similarities and differences.

"How do you feel?" I ask him.

"I feel great," he answers, leaning forward to give me a kiss.

"That's not what I meant. I should word this better. Do you feel different than you did before the experiment?" I clarify.

"I feel stronger. I had a lot of medical issues when I was younger, that I grew out of. I exercised to strengthen my muscles, and it worked, but I was never as strong as I should have been. And now, it is just easier to do things," he answers.

"Oh yeah? What kind of things?" I say with a flirty smirk, moving so I am standing between his legs.

"I don't know. Sometimes I would get winded if I went up the stairs too fast," he answers, my intentions going completely over his head.

I gently grab his chin and tilt his head down to look at me. "I was trying to be sexy, Steve." I point out to him.

"Oh," he says, nodding for a moment until his eyes widen in realization. "OH."

I chuckle at him and bring my lips to his, running my fingers through his hair. We continue making out and his hands make their way down to my ass.

The goat in the corner bleats, shocking us into separating.

"We should probably be trying to figure out what happened to me?" he asks once we have caught our breath.

"You are the one touching my butt," I tease. "Do you remember anything about the experiment?"

He looks past me, his focus turning inward. "I didn't fully lie to you the other day. My last day in 1945 isn't clear. I have a vague idea of what happened and I'm trying to remember things, but I can't see anything specific."

I give him a small peck, bringing him back to himself. "It's okay. We'll figure it out."

The results from the frequency analysis would be enlightening. Seeing how they are different would help us to compare what the time machine did to what was done to Steve. The only problem is that it would take hours for the information to render. Looking on the bright side, it means I have some time to kill with Steve. The smart thing to do would be to remain professional, but that ship has already sailed. My best bet would be to take full advantage of the limited time Steve and I have left.

"What kind of things did you like to do back in the 40s?" I ask.

"Do you think my hobbies might have something to do with the time machine?" Steve asks, looking more confused than when I was trying to flirt with him.

"No, I just picked the last thing we did and thought you should have a turn."

"But what about…" Steve starts but I put my finger up to stop him.

"The computer has to compile the results. It's going to take a while. So, I thought we could spend the afternoon together. No tests. No time machine. No experiments. Just fun. There has got to be something you did that is still around," I explain.

"Ollie and I used to go to the beach a lot. It was a free spot to spend time, so we took full advantage."

"Then let's go to the beach."

He smiles at me. "I don't have a bathing suit."

"Then it's a good thing there are about fifty

places to buy one on the boardwalk."

A few hours later, Steve and I are on the beach, building a sand castle. It's unseasonably warm for January, so the beach is packed with tourists and locals trying to soak up the weather, but we blend in well. I'm wearing my neon pink bikini, and since I couldn't convince Steve to wear a speedo, he's wearing yellow swim trunks with Malibu written across the butt.

I find a small wooden stick in the sand and jam it on the top of our castle. I take a few steps back and tilt my head to the side to admire our architecture. We have mounded the sand into a giant pile with two smaller piles next to it that I think are supposed to be turrets. Steve stands beside me, also looking at our handiwork.

"What is that supposed to be?" he asks, referring to the stick I just added.

"A flag," I answer, as if it is the most obvious thing in the world.

"Right," he says.

"I think it looks great. Maybe not like a castle, but more of a majestic mountain range," I say, gesturing with my arms out wide to really paint the picture.

Steve purses his lips and takes another look. "Or a couple of hills."

"Majestic hills," I correct him.

"When was the last time you made a sand castle?" he asks with one of those perfect smiles of his.

I think about my answer for a while; I have to dig way back in the archives. "Probably when I was six, before my mom died. Eli isn't really a beach guy. That's why the house is on a cliff," I answer. "What about you?"

"Probably just before I enlisted." His smile falls a little bit.

"You went with Ollie?"

He nods. It's bittersweet hearing him talk about Ollie. It's easy to forget that he has a life back home and people that would miss him—that he probably misses.

Steve puts his hand over his eyes to block the sun so he could see clearer. "You should have let me buy you that Dodger's hat. Maybe then you could see the beautiful mountain range we created."

"I told you. It felt wrong that my team isn't in Brooklyn anymore. I can't endorse it."

I shake my head and roll my eyes. "Question. You live near here right? Like in your own time," I ask.

"Yes, not in your fancy neighborhood, but nearby."

"Then why do you cheer for a baseball team from the other side of the country?"

"It was my dad's favourite team. He was from Brooklyn, but back then they were the Robins," he explains.

"It's nice that you can share that with your dad." It's clear on Steve's face that he is still sad about losing his dad. I turn my attention back to our mountain range.

"I think if I add a few more rough edges, that would help sell it as mountains." I drop to my knees and start carving out some details in the sand.

Steve stays standing and I can feel his eyes watching me. He sits down next to me after a few quiet moments and points to my shoulder.

"You have a tattoo," he says. "I didn't notice it last night."

I cringe slightly at the mention of my tattoo. I like to forget it's there; it is kind of embarrassing. The Ace of Hearts on my shoulder. A very basic white girl thing to do.

"Silly, drunk, eighteen-year-old me thought it would bring me love," I explain.

"It still could," he says.

I look into those blue eyes of his and start to lean in for a kiss, but a loud metallic crack distracts me.

Steve and I turn toward the source of the noise. We find it quickly when a child's scream rings out through the air. It's coming from the Ferris wheel on the pier. The car at the very top has its door open and a little boy is hanging on to the handle, dangling perilously.

"I should go help him," Steve says, turning to run up the beach to the pier, but I grab his arm to stop him.

He looks back at me, buzzing and ready to spring into action. "Steve, you can't go up there," I tell him. There are people with phones everywhere waiting to film the rescue, and we can't afford for him to end up on the news.

"Why not?" I haven't told him about Soup yet. I don't want to scare him. I could explain everything now, but the look of pure determination in his eye keeps me from keeping him any longer. It would be selfish of me to tell him not to go.

"Be careful," I say instead, letting go of his arm.

Steve bolts down the beach and over to the pier. He is definitely going faster than a normal person would. I just hope people see his muscular form and just think he's very fit. Just as I thought, a bunch of bystanders on the beach have their phones out. I can hear sirens in the distance and no doubt will there be news crews that follow.

I pick up my beach bag and throw my flip-flops on. I follow where Steve went so I can get him away as soon as the kid is safe. When I make it to the entrance of the pier, I turn my attention to Steve's rescue mission. He has made it to the Ferris wheel and is starting to climb. I stop in my tracks as worry grips me. Yes, Steve is strong, but I feel like it won't help him survive a fall like that.

The little boy is still holding on, but it seems like his grip is slipping. Steve is about halfway up the Ferris wheel now. He is moving quickly but still taking the time to ensure he's placing his hands and feet in the best possible places.

I make my way through the crowd, eyes on Steve the entire time. When he finally makes it to the top, he talks to the boy. They are too high up to hear what they are saying, but I know Steve's warm eyes and bright smile are likely putting the boy at ease.

The tension in the crowd is palpable when Steve reaches out his hand for the boy to take hold of. The hand that isn't holding the car door takes Steve's. Then once the boy has a hold on Steve, he lets go of the car.

There's a collective gasp as the boy's body drops, only to be caught by Steve. He pulls the boy up and tucks him into his body, starting the climb back down. There is a smattering of applause through the crowd, but the climb down is just as dangerous.

I continue to make my way to the front of the crowd. I need to beat the paramedics and news crews that have just arrived. I need to get Steve out of here as soon as he touches the ground.

I'm at the base of the Ferris wheel a few minutes before Steve ends the descent with the boy in his arms. He jumps the last few feet, supporting the boy so he doesn't get hurt, then places the child on his feet.

"Are you okay?" Steve asks the little boy.

"Yeah. Thank you, sir," the boy replies.

A woman breaks through the crowd and wraps the little boy in a giant hug.

I take the opportunity to break from the crowd myself and go to Steve. I give him a quick hug and whisper in his ear. "I'm really glad you and the kid are okay, but we have to go."

I pull back from the hug to find a slightly confused expression on Steve's face. I take his hand and lead him back into the crowd just as the news crews arrive.

"Keep your head down," I instruct Steve, and he follows my lead.

"Sir! Sir! Where are you going? We would love to talk to you about your heroic feat," the journalists start to yell at him.

"No comment," I yell back, just trying to keep us moving forward.

I can only hope that none of the cameras got close to either of our faces.

CHAPTER 16

I stop Steve outside the front door of the mansion. We changed back into our normal clothes in the car, so we have plausible deniability if footage of our eventful day at the beach is already on the news. "Okay, so you're clear on the plan?" I ask him.

"Yes. If Eli asks, we were just out for lunch," he answers. I nod and take a deep breath. Steve puts his hands on my shoulders and looks into my eyes. "Ace, it's going to be fine," he reassures me.

It's hard to find comfort in his words knowing

that he doesn't know the gravity of the situation yet. I nod again and open the door.

Steve follows me in and we try to make our way up the stairs, but Joy is standing at the top with her arms crossed. "Eli wants to see you in the living room," she says with the usual air of disapproval in her voice.

I maintain a calm and collected demeanor as I continue up the stairs, taking Steve by the hand and dragging him along with me. "Eli can wait," I reply as I walk past the housekeeper.

"ACE!" Eli's voice carries from downstairs.

Steve and I stop in our tracks and look at each other. We turn and start heading back down the stairs, walking past a very smug-looking Joy.

The living room, like the rest of the house, is very sleek and modern. There is another wall of floor to ceiling windows that overlook the ocean, but the real focal point of the room is the giant television. The windows were even treated with a special coating to prevent glare on the TV.

Eli is standing in front of said television when Steve and I walk into the living room. On the screen is news footage of Steve's daring rescue.

"So, you decided to have a beach day?" Eli asks, eerily calm.

"A beach day? Why would you think we were at the beach?" I reply.

The news footage continues and Eli pauses on a shot of Steve and I leaving the pier. You could only see our faces for a second, but there we are.

"That could be anybody," I lie.

"Ace, he scaled a Ferris Wheel. Forget Campbell finding out. This could bring down all kinds of unwanted attention on us," Eli argues.

"It's not that big of a deal. Ryan Gosling did it in *The Notebook* and he was just a normal guy," I say.

"I think I'm missing something. Who is Campbell?" Steve asks.

An evil smirk slides across Eli's face. "Looks like someone hasn't been completely honest with her boy toy," he teases.

I glare at Eli before turning to Steve. A pit forms in my stomach at the hurt look in his eye. "I never lied. I just left out some information because I didn't want you to worry," I explain.

"Worry about what, exactly?" Steve asks.

"Can you guys wait to have this argument until

I can grab some popcorn?" Eli interjects.

I throw him another glare before grabbing Steve's hand and taking him upstairs. I lead him all the way to my room and shut the door behind us.

"Can you please tell me what is going on?" Steve asks again.

I take a deep breath, giving myself a minute to figure out exactly where to start. "Lawrence Campbell is a friend of Eli's. He's military and Eli seems to think that he is attempting the same experiments that were done on you in 1945," I explain.

"Why would that worry me?" he asks.

"Because if he finds out who you are and that the experiment worked, he's going to want to study you," I explain.

"Won't he have questions about how I got here? I would think a time machine would be more interesting to him."

"It might, but Eli will give you up before he gives up his time machine." Steve sits on the bed and puts his head in his hands. I kneel in front of him and put a comforting hand on his thigh. "I know this is a lot to take in."

"I just wish you would have told me. Going to the beach today was completely reckless. I should have never suggested it," he says as he puts his hand on mine and looks at me.

"It's fun to be reckless sometimes," I reply with a flirty smile, attempting to keep Steve from beating himself up for something that wasn't his fault.

I can see the corners of his lips turn slightly upward before his practical side takes over again. "I wouldn't have brought attention to myself by rescuing that boy."

"Yes, you would have, and that's a good thing." I take his chin between my fingers and guide his lips to mine. "I really think it's going to be fine. Campbell is only interested in international news. He's not going to care about some rescue on the pier. Plus, you can barely tell it's us."

"Eli figured it out," Steve argues.

"Eli knows you're here. No one is going to watch that and think I bet he's an enhanced soldier from 1945," I reply.

I lean in to kiss him again, but stop when I hear the doorbell. "Are you expecting someone?" Steve asks.

"No," I reply.

It is extremely weird for the doorbell to ring. One of Eli's eccentric billionaire tendencies was that he didn't want people to know where he lived. He even has Joy pick up all his mail from another house he owns. "You stay here. I'm going to go check it out."

I head down the stairs to find the last person I expected standing in the foyer next to Joy. "Sawyer, what are you doing here?" I ask.

"I need to talk to you. In private," he says, signalling to Joy with his eyes. "Can we go up to your room?"

"No. Joy, can you give us a minute?" I ask the housekeeper. She nods and gets the heck out of dodge. "What do you want?"

"I saw you on the news," he answers.

I keep my face neutral, even though this could be very bad. There is no way Sawyer knows anything. He doesn't even know what Soup is working on. "I was on the news?" Denial seemed to be the best route to go here.

"Come on, Ace. I know that neon pink bikini and silly card tattoo anywhere." I block out all the memories of him peeling off that bikini and kissing that tattoo in the throes of passion. I'm not about to let him distract me.

"That still doesn't tell me why you are here," I say.

"Who was that guy you were with?" he asks.

"Why? Are you jealous?" I clap back.

He steps closer to me and lowers his voice. "Is he one of Campbell's test subjects?" he asks.

"What?" I have to tread carefully now. Sawyer can't know he's on the right track. He's a wild card and would definitely go straight to Soup with whatever knowledge he thinks he has.

"I broke into Campbell's office yesterday. I saw the folder with the Ferris wheel guy's picture in it. He is working on an enhanced soldier program. But of course, you already know that since you are clearly taking his little pets out for walks." He's getting heated, so he turns away and takes a step to cool off a bit.

"Do you hear yourself? If you're jealous that I'm with someone else, you can just say that. You don't need to go making up ridiculous theories," I say.

He whips back around and takes another step towards me. He grabs my arm hard and pulls me towards him to close the gap. "Tell me the truth, Ace," he orders, right in my face.

"I suggest you take your hands off of her." A stern voice comes from the top of the stairs. Sawyer drops my arm and looks over my head at the man now making his way toward us.

"Who the hell are you?" Sawyer asks as Steve stands behind me, putting his arm around my waist and pulling me into him.

"I'm her boyfriend. Who are you?" I try not to look shocked. I've never had a man refer to himself as my boyfriend before.

"He's nobody," I answer before Sawyer can. "You should go now, Sawyer."

"You said that you would tell me if you knew what Campbell was up to. Don't act like I'm the bad guy here."

This is Sawyer's game. Make everything my fault. I'm the one who misinterpreted the signals that he wasn't giving me. I'm the one who thought we were more than just sex. I'm the one jeopardizing his career. Well, now I'm the one who has had enough.

"What happened at the beach today has nothing to do with Campbell. Please leave," I say calmly.

"But, Ace—" Sawyer starts, but Steve cuts him off.

"She told you to leave," he says, his stern tone vibrating through his chest. "Can you follow that simple instruction, or am I going to have to show you out?"

Sawyer gives Steve a glare as he turns around and leaves.

I let out a breath I didn't know I was holding and turn around in Steve's arms to face him.

"Boyfriend, huh?" I say to him with a little smirk.

Steve immediately blushes. "I just thought that..." he blurts out in a panic.

I stop his rambling with a finger to his lips. "It's okay. I liked it."

"You did?" he asks.

I wrap my arms around his neck and nod. "In fact, I found the whole coming to my rescue thing incredibly hot." I watch with satisfaction as his Adam's apple bobs. "I think we should go to bed early."

"It has been a long day." I giggle a little at Steve's naivety.

"Well, I hope you're not too tired because I was talking about having sex." His eyes widen, but I can see the heat in them. I pull him for a kiss and wrap my legs around his waist. "Let's go upstairs."

CHAPTER 17

I lie in bed awake, looking at the stars through the skylight. Steve cleaned up all the splinters from our incident the night before, so we're back to sleeping in my room. When I moved into the house, I picked this room specifically for the skylight. Yes, the sun shining through it made for an earlier wake up time, but it's worth it for the view of the night sky when I can't sleep.

I turn to look at Steve. It should be illegal for someone to look that good when they are asleep. I should be upset that he is sleeping while I'm lying awake worried about him, but I'm more relieved that he is calm enough to sleep. He's been through a lot in the last few days.

I'm also the one who told him everything would be fine. At the time I believed it, but Sawyer showing up threw me. Now that he is convinced he has all the evidence he needs it would be just like him to go confront Soup and, in turn, lead him straight to us.

I turn again because looking at Steve is just making my mind race more. I look at the phone on my nightstand and it lights up with a notification. I pick it up and look at the screen. There's a text from Sawyer. It says, "Campbell confirmed everything. I'm so glad we never dated. I dodged a bullet."

I stare at the text. This isn't good. This is really, really, not good. I need to make a call, but my damn boyfriend has super hearing. I start to slowly slip out of the bed.

As soon as my feet hit the floor, a voice comes from the other side of the bed. "Where are you going?" Steve asks.

"Just going to get a glass of water."

He grunts in acknowledgement and rolls over. I wait for his breathing to even out again. I know he can hear me from downstairs, but if he's asleep and I am all the way down in the kitchen, I might be okay. Also, my room is soundproofed and the guest room isn't.

I get down to the kitchen and dial the number. He answers on the first ring, like he's been expecting my call. "Ace, it's late for you to be calling me. I thought you would be asleep since you had such an eventful day on the beach," Soup says on the other end of the line.

I take a deep breath before I respond. "What do you want?" I ask, keeping my voice steady even though inside I was anything but.

"You know what I want."

"I'll help you with your project. Steve just needs to stay out of it." It's getting harder to keep the desperation out of my voice and from the chuckle that goes through the phone, he can probably tell.

"You are overplaying your hand, Ace. He must be good in bed."

"Bold of you to assume I'm sleeping with him."

"I've seen him. A man like that gets hand

delivered to your house, there is no way you aren't fucking him."

"Campbell. What do you want?" I plead, calling him by his preferred name for the first time in years.

"Nothing you are able or willing to offer," he responds coldly.

"Come on, you've known me since I was six. I've never asked you for anything. Please, don't take him away from me." I hold back my tears. I'm already begging. I don't need to give him the satisfaction of making me cry.

"Yes, you have, and I gave it to you. Then you blew it for a different dick."

"Please."

"Good night, Ace. Enjoy your new toy while you still can." The line goes dead.

I put the phone down on the counter and take a minute to compose myself. The best thing I can do now is go back to Steve. Get as much time as I can with him.

I head up the stairs and crawl back into bed. I close my eyes to try to employ a fake it until you make it approach to sleep, when I feel two strong arms wrap around my waist and pull me into a strong chest. "Why can't you sleep?" Steve whispers into my ear.

"I just can't turn my brain off," I answer, not lying, just not telling the full truth.

"Grab your phone," Steve says, and I follow his order, picking up my phone from where I had just put it back on the nightstand. I hold it up so we can both see the time on the lock screen. It's 12:03.

Steve gives me a kiss on my temple and says, "It's midnight. You made it to tomorrow. There is nothing else to worry about."

I put my phone back down and turn in his arms to face him. "I like spending midnights with you," I tell him, and wrap my arms around his neck, pulling him in for a kiss.

I move my hand to his shoulder and shift to move to my back and tug him with me. He breaks from the kiss and looks at me with his eyebrows raised. "Ace, we already did that, and it didn't seem to help you sleep," he says.

"Well, we can always try again and see if it will work this time," I argue and bring his lips to mine once again.

This time, he gives in.

He's lying on top of me as we make out. His hands start to make their way down my body, but they stop before they hit their target. He pulls away from the kiss and looks around the room. "Did you hear that?" he asks.

"Hear what?" I say, and he puts a finger to my lips, signaling me to be quiet.

He slowly sits up, carefully listening to whatever his heightened senses are picking up.

"Get under the bed," he says, getting out of the bed and standing next to it. His entire body is tense and on alert. It scares me enough that I do what he says and slide under the bed.

From my vantage point, all I can see are Steve's feet. Just when I start to think he may have overreacted, I hear a crash and see three sets of combat boots join Steve's bare feet. I throw my hand over my mouth to keep from screaming.

All I can hear are the grunts of exertion and I try not to let my mind fill in the details with Steve losing. There are sharp clangs as three guns hit the floor one after the other. One has landed just a little out of my reach. Based on the noises I'm hearing, our guests are distracted and are not likely to notice a hand sliding out from under the bed and grabbing the gun.

I slip along the floor and slowly reach for the gun. Before I can grab it, I hear the telltale sound of a body hitting the floor. I turn to make sure it's not Steve and breathe a sigh of relief when I see a man in tactical gear lying on the floor. I look back to where my hand is a moment too late. One of the other men grabs my wrist and pulls me out from under the bed and up onto my feet. He tries to pull me into him, but I elbow him in the groin. He lets go of me in reaction, and I launch myself on to the bed to get away.

I glance toward Steve, who has the second man in a sleeper hold. He passes out and Steve turns his attention to the man coming after me. Steve leads with a punch to the face that the man blocks, leaving him distracted enough for Steve to deliver his second punch to the man's gut. He buckles at the impact and Steve makes use of his prone position and brings his fist hard into the man's face, knocking him out.

Once he's sure the man is down, Steve comes over to check on me. "Ace, are you okay?" he asks, taking my face in his hands.

I look down to assess and find that I have a few cuts on my arms. Looking around the room, it looks like they are from landing on the glass that was all over the bed from the assailants coming through the windows and skylight.

"I'm fine," I answer Steve as he helps me off the bed so I don't get cut again.

I step carefully around the men on the floor, taking in their features. They look familiar, but I can't immediately place them. Then I see the scar on one of their eyes. "I know these guys."

"Campbell?" Steve asks.

I nod. "They are part of his special task force. I've seen them around the base." The men aren't dead, just unconscious. There's no telling how long it'll take them to wake up. "We should tie them up before they come to." I open the door so we can start getting them out of here.

"What?" Steve asks.

"What do you mean what? We tie them up. Then we call Soup and tell him he can have his guys back when he agrees to leave us alone," I explain.

"Ace, we can't take them as hostages. And who

is Soup?" he argues.

"Campbell is Soup," I explain, and he nods, putting together my clever nickname. "What do you think we should do with them? Let them go so they can come back tomorrow night and break another window. I don't think Eli would be happy about that."

"What wouldn't I be happy about?" Eli says as he appears at the bedroom door as if summoned by the mention of his name. He looks around the room like he just realized the chaos that ensued. "What the hell happened here?"

"What does it look like?" I bark out.

"We have to let them go, Ace. We can talk to Campbell. I'm sure we can come to a reasonable agreement and the men won't be back tomorrow," Steve says, ignoring Eli.

Eli isn't a fan of being ignored, so butts his way into the room and stands between Steve and I. "This is still my house. Someone care to explain to me the property damage."

"Soup sent his special ops team to get Steve."

Eli doesn't react right away. His expression turns blank, and he gets very serious.

"I'll talk to Campbell. These men will not be

back. Put them outside. They can find their own way home," Eli orders, then leaves the room.

Steve starts to pick up the first man but I run to follow Eli. "What are you going to say to Soup?" I ask.

Eli stops and turns around, walking back towards me. "None of your damn business. We tried this your way, Ace. It's my turn now," he says, and heads back the way he came.

I just stand and watch as he goes into his room and shuts the door behind him.

CHAPTER 18

Sundays are Joy's day off. Usually, I go out to breakfast with Natalie, but with everything going on with Steve, I cancelled our weekly ritual. Instead, I decide to make breakfast myself.

The hash browns are cooking in the air fryer. The Pop-Tarts are toasting in the toaster and I have my Taylor Swift playlist on full blast. With the heaviness of everything that happened last night, the only cure is Taylor. I'm jamming out to the bridge of "Cruel Summer," complete with choreography and ladle microphone, when Steve enters the kitchen. He stops and watches me as I serenade him with Taylor's poetic words. I dance over to him and grab his hand so he'll dance with me.

He begrudgingly follows me. "What is this?" he asks.

"Music," I answer.

"I know that. It's just a little different from what I'm used to," he clarifies.

I grab my phone off the counter and pause the music. "This is Taylor Swift. She's an icon. She's a phenomenon. Like the Beatles," I explain.

"Who are the Beatles?" he asks, still confused.

"Wow, you really are old," I tease. Steve rolls his eyes at me. I turn around to fetch the hash browns from the air fryer. "Do you want some breakfast?" I ask.

"Did you make enough for all of us?" asks a familiar voice that does not belong to Steve. The sound of it makes a chill go down my spine.

I take a breath to build up my armour and I turn back around to find Soup and Eli standing in the archway that separates the kitchen from the foyer. "What the hell are you doing here? Come to assess the damage you caused in my room?" I ask.

"Bold of you to be upset about damage to a house that doesn't actually belong to you," Eli chimes in.

"I've apologized to Eli for that. Based on my phone call with him, I went through too much trouble. It turns out all I had to do was ask," Soup explains.

A pit forms in my stomach. I move around the island and put myself between Steve and the two other men. "Your first idea was really kidnapping?" I ask, keeping my tone snarky to hide my very real fear.

"Well, based on the conversation I had with you last night, I deduce that your guest has been here for a while. You seem rather attached to the enhanced soldier you two somehow acquired from 1945."

"What makes you think that Steve is from 1945?" Playing dumb seems like the best move right now. Even though it is likely Eli has already confirmed his suspicion.

"I have a file in my office with Steve's picture in it. Looks like it was taken yesterday. Which, I guess for him, it was, wasn't it?"

Eli and I look at each other. "I mean, if we want to split hairs, he's been here for three nights," I say quietly.

Soup turns his focus to Eli. "You built the time machine, didn't you? You built the fucking time machine, and you didn't tell me! I am your best friend."

"Best friend seems like a strong word," I interject, a little louder than intended.

"Ace. I swear to god if I hear one more snarky remark out of you…" He trails off as Steve takes a step forward to get in front of me.

"If you want to get to her, you will have to go through me," Steve says.

Soup's lips turn up in a wicked grin. "So, you really are fucking him. I was just guessing last night. I'm not surprised, though. You'll fuck anything with a pulse. If your performance is inspiring this kind of protectiveness, you must be pretty good."

"Wouldn't you like to know," I retort.

"Not even with the world's thickest condom."

This time, Steve has to hold me back as I attempt to lunge at Soup. I look at him and he looks back at me with a calming expression.

"That's enough." I hear Eli scold but can't see exactly who he is talking to.

I pull myself together long enough to ask, "What do you want, Soup?"

"I want the technological advancement that I am owed. Honestly, I don't really care whether that is in the form of your new sex doll or the time machine. That is up to you and Eli," he answers.

I step in front of Steve. It's my turn to be the protective one. "We aren't going to just give you Steve. He's a human being."

"You see, that's where you are wrong," Soup says as he moves closer to me. "According to my files, *Steve* went missing in 1945. Which means the man standing behind you doesn't actually exist. Which, in turn, means I can do whatever the hell I want with him."

I take a step back, closer to Steve, and put my hand behind me to hold his. My eyes go to Eli, but he has his down. "Take him," he says.

"Absolutely fucking not," I argue.

"I really don't think that's your decision," Soup counters. "Of course, I can send my men to come get him. With Eli's cooperation, I'm sure all they will have to do is subdue you."

"I'd like to see them try," I say, taking a step closer to Soup, getting right in his face.

I feel Steve's hand on my shoulder, pulling me back.

"I'll go with you," Steve says. I turn to face him and open my mouth to object, but he puts his hand up to stop me. "Just give me one more day with Ace."

"So that you and her can run away together, I don't think so."

"If we run away, you'll send your men after us, right? If my goal here is to protect Ace, then it wouldn't make sense to run."

I look back at Soup, who shrugs. "Fine. I'm getting bored with this anyway. I guess I will see you all tomorrow." He heads out of the kitchen, leaving Eli, Steve and I standing there.

"Are those Pop-Tarts up for grabs?" Eli asks, breaking the silence. He goes over to the toaster and grabs the long forgotten pastries.

"That's all you are going to say? Soup is about to take away the one person that cares about me and you're worried about the Pop-Tarts."

It's the last straw for me with Eli. I've done

everything he asked, but he doesn't care about me enough to put me over his stupid time machine.

"You think I don't care about you? Look around, kid. I paid for the best education, gave you a job at my company, kept a roof over your head—a pretty extravagant one, in fact. What more do you want from me?" Eli argues.

"I never asked for any of that. I didn't need your boarding schools or your mansion. I needed a dad," I yell back.

I storm out of the room. I'm not about to waste my last day with Steve arguing with Eli.

Steve follows me out of the kitchen and catches me before I start going up the stairs. "Are you okay?" he asks, holding my shoulders, crouching so he can look in my eyes.

"No," I tell him. I take a deep breath and think about the predicament we are in. "I want to take you somewhere."

"Anywhere," he answers.

Steve is quiet as I drive him through a quaint suburban neighbourhood. We drive past white picket fences that contain children playing on pristinely green lawns. I pull into the driveway of one of the houses.

It's the smallest house on the street, and definitely the most eclectic. The siding is a dark blue with white trim. There is a little porch at the front with red rocking chairs that match the red front door. The peak of the roof has a window that opens to a small balcony, only big enough for two.

Steve and I get out of the car and he looks at me. "What is this place?" he asks.

"It's my house," I say, offering no further explanation before heading up the porch steps.

Steve catches up to me as I'm knocking. The door opens to reveal a woman who, if you squint, can easily be mistaken for me. She has the same shade of auburn hair and similar hazel eyes. She smiles when she sees me and steps outside to wrap me in a hug.

"Hi, Ace," I say.

"Hi, sweetie," the other Ace replies.

I take a peek at Steve, whose brow is becoming more furrowed in confusion by the second. She follows my gaze and notices that I'm not alone. "Who's the hottie?" she whispers to me loud enough that Steve would be able to hear her even without heightened senses.

"Oh, just some guy. Do you mind if I borrow your balcony again?" I ask.

The other Ace takes a step back and gestures for us to come in. "Come on in. Mi casa is quite literally su casa."

I roll my eyes and walk past her into the house.

Steve follows me in. The place is furnished in trendy furniture but is still warm and cozy. I head up the staircase on the side of the foyer. I go to the end of the hallway at the top of the stairs, where there is a string dangling from the ceiling. I pull the string, revealing a ladder. Steve and I head up the ladder into the small attic.

The attic is unfinished, and Steve has to duck a little because the ceiling is low. There is a large window on one wall and we head towards it. I open the window and climb out onto the small balcony.

All that can be seen from the front of the house is the railing, but stepping out onto the balcony, it's bigger than it looks. There are two chairs and a small table, very simple, but the real draw of the balcony is the view. You can see the whole neighbourhood. All the slightly differentiated from each other houses lined up in neat little rows with happy little families living inside.

I sit in one of the chairs and Steve sits in the other. I can see him holding in his questions, trying to be polite. I take a few minutes to take in the view before putting him out of his misery. "Her real name is Jess. She's my decoy," I explain.

"Your decoy?" Steve asks, looking no less confused.

"Eli is terrified of assassination and kidnapping attempts, so very few people have his actual home address. He owns another house that all his mail goes to. He's recognizable, so no one lives there. When I started at the company, Eli bought this place in my name. He also hired Jess. If someone comes to the office asking for me without an appointment, she's the one they send out. She lives here and everyone in the neighbourhood knows her as Ace."

"Has anything ever happened?" he asks.

"No, Eli is just paranoid. There are probably a lot of holes in his system, but I like having this place to get away to, so I just let it be." I look out at the neighbourhood again and take a deep sigh.

Steve moves his chair closer to mine and takes my hand. "It is pretty peaceful up here," he says.

I rest my head on his shoulder, and we sit in comfortable silence for a few moments. "You didn't tell me you talked to Campbell last night."

I turn my head to look at him. "When you were asleep Sawyer texted me and said he'd talked to Soup," I explain.

"What does texted mean?"

I fight the urge to giggle at his question. "A text is like a short written message you send to someone's phone."

"Oh." Steve nods but I can tell he doesn't fully grasp the concept. I also get the feeling that he is more interested in what I have kept from him than new technology.

"I called Soup to try and get him not to take you. I practically begged him but you saw him today. He doesn't give a shit about anyone but himself, and the best thing for him would be to turn you into an experiment."

I pause for a moment and Steve kisses me on the forehead. He's quiet again for a moment and I can tell something is still bothering him. "Penny for your thoughts," I say.

"Is the only reason you want me to stick around because of the sex?"

I sit up in my chair and whip towards him. "Of course not. I mean don't get me wrong, the sex is great but I like you."

"Okay. I just thought with what Campbell said about you…you know with anything with a pulse, that maybe you just thought I was handsome or something." His eyes are on his fingers as he fiddles with the hem of his shirt.

"Steve. Look at me." He flits his gaze back to me. "I like sex. I make no apologies for that. But with you, it's more than that. I didn't want to sleep with you, I knew I would get attached. But something about you reeled me in. You make me feel safe and I never thought I would have that. Do you know why I come up here?"

"Because of the view?" he guesses.

"Kind of. I come up here because I like to watch the happy little families in their normal lives. I've never had anything like that so I come up here and play make believe. I make up little stories about the little families and pretend they are mine. But with you I don't have to pretend. I feel like I finally have what I have been missing, someone that cares about me."

The corners of his lips pull up as he takes my hand and guides me to go sit in his lap. I lean into his chest as he whispers to me. "You've broken my walls down, too. And I'm so grateful you did."

We stay sitting together like that for a while. I

breathe in his scent and tune out everything around me except for him. The sun lowers in the sky and it reminds me of the passage of time, the limited amount I have left with him. I want to know everything about him.

"What is your mom like?" I ask while absent-mindedly tracing the pattern of his shirt with my finger.

"She's the hardest worker I know, but never let that get in the way of family. Especially after we took Ollie in. The one thing I remember most from my childhood is that she would read to me before bed every night. She's a nurse, so has to work odd shifts. But we live so close to the hospital that if she was working, she would time her breaks so that she could come home and read to me," he answers. "What was yours like?"

"I remember the odd little details. We have the same colour eyes. Her favourite food was watermelon. Silly things like that. But the thing I remember most is that she loved me." I take a deep breath. I never talk about my mom. Hardly anyone has ever asked about her. I turn to face Steve and he is watching me, hanging on my every word. His blue eyes radiating that comfort that makes talking to him easy. How am I supposed to let him go?

The thought of losing him is eating away at me, so I ask the question that I have been avoiding all day. "Why did you tell Soup you would go with him?"

He shifts his gaze to our joined hands, breaking eye contact with me. "He threatened you." He opens his mouth to say something else but stops.

I place my finger under his chin and bring his gaze back to mine. "I can take care of myself. You're really willing to resign yourself to experiments for me?"

He shrugs. "It felt like the right thing to do."

I try not to let my disappointment show. I really thought he was going to say it was because he loved me. But I shouldn't have expected that. Steve and I have only known each other for a few days. We aren't in love. Not yet, but maybe if I could find a way to keep him here.

"Campbell really seems to hate you," he says.

"The feeling is mutual."

"Sounds like there is a story there."

He's right. There is a story. A raw and

vulnerable one that I have never told before in its entirety. Natalie knew pieces, but I never told her the whole thing. But I'm not worried, I have been telling Steve everything about my life, why stop now?

"After I graduated from college, I decided I wanted to rebel by joining the military. Soup got me a job with a trial unit of men with Cosimo prosthetics," I begin my story.

"What is a Cosimo prosthetic?"

"It's a prosthetic limb that moves using neuro…" I trail off and adjust my wording based on the confusion on Steve's face. "It moves with signals from the brain. Eli invented them and the program Soup started would hopefully give soldiers that lost a limb a chance to serve their country again."

"That's a pretty admirable thing."

"Too bad it wasn't about the soldiers and just about Soup making himself look better."

"Is that what happened between you two?"

"The Captain of the unit didn't have a prosthetic. He was brought in to oversee us all. He told me how much he admired me and all the other things a girl wants to hear. One day, it went a little too far, and we ended up in bed together. We started hooking up regularly and then one day, Soup found out. He brought me into his office and said that he dodged my sabotaging of his career once that he wasn't about to let me succeed this time."

"You sabotaged his career?"

"Exactly my question. He said the first time was when I showed up at Eli's door."

"You were six."

"I was indeed. Turns out, it was Soup's idea to claim I was Eli's cousin. He said it would look better to the public if he took in a family member who didn't have anyone else. Having a child he knew nothing about made him look irresponsible. His career is tied to Eli's. He brought Eli's technology to the military and was rewarded for it handsomely. But if the public opinion of Eli was to take a turn, Soup would go down with the ship." I take a deep breath. It's still a hard memory to talk about. Finding out that Soup was basically responsible for my father essentially disowning me was rough, but that's not the end of the story.

"I left the military after that. I didn't want to work with Soup anymore, and I naively thought that the only thing keeping Sawyer and I apart was that we needed to be a secret. Turns out he never actually thought of us as a couple."

"The same Sawyer who showed up last night?" Steve asks.

"Yup. That one." We should have brought some drinks up here. This would be better with tequila.

Steve put his arm around me and kissed the top of my head. "Well, he's clearly an idiot. He missed out on someone amazing."

I turn my head and take in the beautiful man I've been too foolish to stay away from. "There has got to be a way around this," I tell him.

"You could just send me back," Steve suggests, and it feels like a dagger to the heart. After all this, he still wants to go back.

"What do you mean?" I reply.

"If I go back, then there is no incident. The experiment is successful, and Campbell doesn't have to pick it up again." If this was *Back to the Future*, that solution would make sense, but this is real life.

"I don't think it works like that."

"How do you know?" he asks, not in challenge but as a genuine question.

"Steve, Soup has been working on these experiments for a while, before the time machine even existed. Besides, we still haven't figured out if it is even safe for you to go back."

My justification sticks out in my mind. If Soup had the files before the time machine, that means Steve was supposed to come back in time. The 1945 part of this story already happened. Maybe this is all meant to happen and Steve does stay. Maybe our future isn't as doomed as I thought it was. Maybe I just need to buy us more time.

With this revelation, pieces seem to fall into place.

"Wait, I think I have an idea."

I once again find myself unable to sleep, heading down to the kitchen in the middle of the night. Only this time, when I get down there, I'm not alone.

Eli is sitting at the island eating a bowl of cereal. He looks at me as I walk in, and once I see him, I turn to go back upstairs.

"Ace, please don't leave because of me. I already ruined your childhood, I don't want to ruin your late night snack." I whip back around and shoot him my best unimpressed look. "I promise I won't even talk to you."

I sigh, and walk back into the kitchen. I open the cupboard, pull out the cereal and pour it in a bowl. The whole time, Eli is surprisingly silent. I take my snack and sit at the opposite end of the island.

We sit quietly for a few minutes. The only sounds are us chewing on the crunchy cereal. I glance over at Eli, he's cringing as he chews, like having to be quiet physically pains him.

"You can talk if you want," I say, putting him out of his misery.

"Thank God." His relief is palpable. "So, your boyfriend didn't want a late-night snack."

"He already had one."

"Eww. I'm your dad, Ace. I don't need to hear that," he replies, gagging dramatically.

I chuckle slightly, and look down at my food. "I think that is the first time you have ever admitted it."

Eli is an expert deflector of awkward conversations, so he replies with, "You really like the guy, don't you?"

"I think I might be in love with him, but I'll never know. Unless Soup's heart grows two sizes and he accepts the proposition I have for him."

"You have a proposition for him?"

"Like you care."

"Maybe I do."

"I'm not giving you all the details to blab to him, but I came up with something reasonable that we all might be able to agree on. But we both know Soup is an unreasonable man, and he's not happy winning unless everyone else loses."

Eli is weirdly quiet and takes another bite of his food. "Maybe he'll surprise you."

I finish my cereal and bring my bowl to the sink. Before I leave the kitchen, Eli speaks again. "Ace, are you sure you might be in love with Steve?"

"I've never been more sure of something." He doesn't turn back to look at me, he just nods and continues eating. I leave the kitchen to go to sleep in my man's arms one last time.

"You're alright with this, right?" I ask Steve before we go into the lion's den. Soup is in the kitchen with Eli waiting for us. Well, they're waiting for Steve. I don't think either of them care if I show up or not.

"Yes, I trust you," he answers.

I lean in to give him a deep kiss. I tossed and turned most of the night, hoping that my solution will work. There is no logical reason why it shouldn't work, the only issue being that it banks on certain people only knowing certain parts of the plan.

I lead Steve into the kitchen. Upon seeing us, Soup stands up and buttons his suit jacket smugly, like he's ready to leave with Steve. "Did you say a proper goodbye?" he asks with a smirk.

"Steve isn't going with you. I have another solution," I say.

He sits back down and puts out his hands in invitation. "I'm all ears."

"You want a Cosimo in on your enhanced soldiers project, right?" Soup nods. "I'll do it. But I'll do it here and my subject will be Steve." I look at the man in question and he looks a little worried. I give him a small, reassuring smile. "I'll figure out what exactly they did to him so you can recreate it on your own soldiers."

"That's it? I'm supposed to just wait for you to figure it out. Why would I agree to that when I can just take him now?" Soup asks.

"Steve will join your special ops team. He was going to be special ops in 1945. He may need some updated training, but he will be an asset to your team," I explain.

Soup narrows his eyes, considering the proposal. He looks from me to Steve to where our hands are joined. He turns to Eli before opening his mouth to answer. I brace myself for the no, but it doesn't come. "I have to hand it to you, Ace. That is definitely an agreeable solution." I try not to let his compliment go to my head. "Make sure your boy toy is ready to report at 0800 hours on Monday." *There's the real Soup.*

He stands up, ready to leave, but something doesn't feel right. It's almost too easy. "You agree? Just like that?" I ask.

Soup walks over to me. He stands close enough that I need to look up at him. I hold my ground, aware of his attempt at intimidation and not letting it get to me. I feel Steve tense at my side, ready to jump in if I'm in trouble. "Well, I trust that you know the consequences should you not hold up your end of the bargain," Soup threatens.

"I guess that makes sense," I reply, making sure to keep my voice light.

He gives me one last glare before turning to Steve. "I'll see you Monday," he says before leaving.

I move to head out of the kitchen, but Eli cuts me off. He waits for the sound of the front door closing before he looks down at me. "What game are you playing at here?" he asks.

"I don't know what you are talking about," I say, and try to move past him, but he cuts me off again.

"Ace, I know you think I don't give a shit about you, but I do. Campbell is not the kind of guy you play games with," he says. I've never seen him so serious.

"I'm not playing a game. I'm going to figure out what happened to Steve, but I'm going to use it to get the time machine to work and send him home," I explain.

"This is a risky play, Ace," he replies.

"I know." I look up at Steve. "But it's worth it."

The part I didn't share with either of the men is that the real play doesn't involve the time machine or the experiments. Both are excuses to buy more time with Steve.

Steve sees me in a way no one else ever has. He is the best thing that has ever happened to me, and I'm not going to let him go without a fight. This was really about buying us more time. Soon he'll fall in love with me, and I won't have to worry about him leaving me.

"We should get working on the time machine then," Eli says, pulling me from my thoughts. "I almost have it ready for another test."

"Another test?" I ask, feeling Steve tense beside me again. If a test makes him this worried, maybe he isn't as eager to leave as I thought.

"Yes, while you two were off gallivanting yesterday, I was using the info we collected from Steve to make some adjustments," Eli explains.

"Are you sure it's a good idea to test again with such little information?" Steve asks.

"Tell you what, old man, if you can figure out how to turn on my television, I'll take your advice on the time machine," Eli quips.

"Eli. He's not totally wrong," I say.

"Whatever, just be ready for a test soon." Eli says, then bolts into the basement, leaving Steve and

I alone.

I turn to Steve and wrapped my arms around his neck. "Any particular reason you don't want us to test the time machine?" I ask.

"Nope, just worried about you," he answers, but there is something off about it.

Before I can scrutinize his sentence, he pulls me in for a kiss that pushes all rational thought out of my brain.

CHAPTER 21

The second goat, Harold, has been mopey ever since the last test of the time machine. I almost feel guilty taking his little rope leash and leading him into the time machine. Once he's on the platform, I kneel to get on his level and give him a little pat on the head. "Don't worry, Harold. Everything is going to be fine. If you see Gerald over there, bring him back with you, okay?" I ask.

Harold bleats in response, and I take it as a yes. I stand up and take my spot next to Eli.

I'm nervous. Steve's reservations about us testing the time machine are giving me pause. He won't tell me what's going on, but something in my gut is telling me we shouldn't be doing this. My feelings are mixed. I want Harold to be safe and, in theory, I want the time machine to work this time. However, if the time machine does work, it means that Steve can leave. He's currently upstairs asleep. Eli wouldn't let me wake him up in case he interfered.

"Subject is in position?" Eli asks.

"His name is Harold," I correct.

"Harold and Gerald?" he asks with a sideways glance.

I glare back at him. "It's adorable."

He rolls his eyes. "Harold is in position?"

"Check," I confirm.

"Destination date and time have been entered correctly in the panel?"

"Check. Are you sure you want to use the same date and time as last time?" I ask.

"Well, Steve's already here, so it is not like that mistake will happen again."

His logic seems sound, so I nod and let him continue. He pushes a few buttons and the time machine whirs to life once again.

"Three…two…one…" Eli counts down and then hits one last button. A flare of light beams from the arms of the machine and when they dim, Harold is gone.

This time we don't celebrate too early. We hold our breath while Eli turns a dial on the control pad and hits another button. The time machine whirs again, but this time the lights don't come on. The whirring slows gradually until it stops all together. No sign of Harold.

I turn to Eli, who is frantically typing. His face slowly looking more and more panicked.

"Did it bring him back somewhere else?" I ask.

Eli stops typing and runs his hands through his hair.

"I think so. His signal popped up for a minute and then disappeared." We just released a time travelling goat into the world. Great.

"Who's signal?" Steve asks, appearing in the doorway.

Eli glares at me and whispers to me. "I thought I told you to lock the door?"

"We never lock that door, and I'm not about to

start now."

Eli and I turn to look at Steve and our distress must clear on our faces, because Steve's bright smile falls when he sees us. "We tested the time machine again. It looks like Harold came back, but we lost his signal so we can't find him," I explain.

Steve rushes over to look at the screen, looking more panicked than we do. "What time did you send him to?" he asks.

"The same one as last time." Steve tenses at my answer. I rub his shoulder to comfort him. "It's okay. Harold is just a goat. We will find him."

Steve turns to face me. Panic and worry filling his blue eyes. "I don't think you brought back Harold."

I have a feeling I know where this is going. I try my best not to freak out before I have all the information. "Babe, what aren't you telling me?"

"You remember my friend Ollie that I told you about?" I nod. "He was getting experimented on at the same time as me."

I let the reality of Steve's words set in. Eli recalibrated the machine to be more sensitive to the correct frequency, but Steve's frequency is so similar to the one the time machine tracks that there is a good chance it would be picked up again, but since Steve is here already we weren't worried about it.

Maybe we should have been because there is a strong possibility that Eli and I brought another time traveller here.

Only this time, we have no idea where to find him.

EPILOGUE

Meanwhile on a farm in 1945

I don't know what we did to get so lucky. As I sit here petting the little brown goat that changed our lives, I can't help but reflect on the whirlwind that has been the last week.

My husband and I have been having a rough time lately. We just can't draw enough visitors to our farm. Usually, enough customers come to our fruit stand to cover our other expenses, but lately we haven't been able to sell the produce before it goes bad.

That was until our friend from the city called and told us that there was a goat that had appeared in the alley next to his shop in a beam of light.

We went to pick up the little guy and he seemed to be in good health, so we took him home.

Word quickly spread about the magical goat and soon people were coming out in droves to get a glimpse of him.

While they were here, they would get hungry, so soon we were selling out of produce completely. We had to resort to charging admission to see the goat. As well as baking pies with the over-ripe fruit we couldn't sell.

I was sure the novelty of the mysterious goat would wear off soon, but, as if answering my fears, today we got another call.

A second goat had appeared in the alley. My husband is away getting him right now.

"You are going to get a new little friend today." I say to the first goat. I swear his little eyes lit up.

I can't help but wonder if he knew the other goat. If they came from the same place.

I like to think that wherever they came from wasn't terrible but was worse than here. I really hope that we are giving them a better life, especially since they are giving us one.

9 781738 022410